Eagles' Revenge

Also by **Roger Mortimer**

Eagle Warrior

ROGER MORTIMER

Eagles' Revenge

mammoth

To Jane, Mark, Susannah and Katie

First published in Great Britain in 2000 by Mammoth,
an imprint of Egmont Children's Books Limited,
239 Kensington High Street, London W8 6SA

Text copyright © 2000 Roger Mortimer
Illustrations copyright © 2000 Neil Roe

The moral rights of the author and illustrator have been asserted.

ISBN 0 7497 3812 X

10 9 8 7 6 5 4 3 2 1

A CIP catalogue record for this title is available from the British Library

Typeset by Avon Dataset Ltd, Bidford on Avon, B50 4JH
Printed in Great Britain by Cox & Wyman Ltd, Reading, Berkshire

Contents

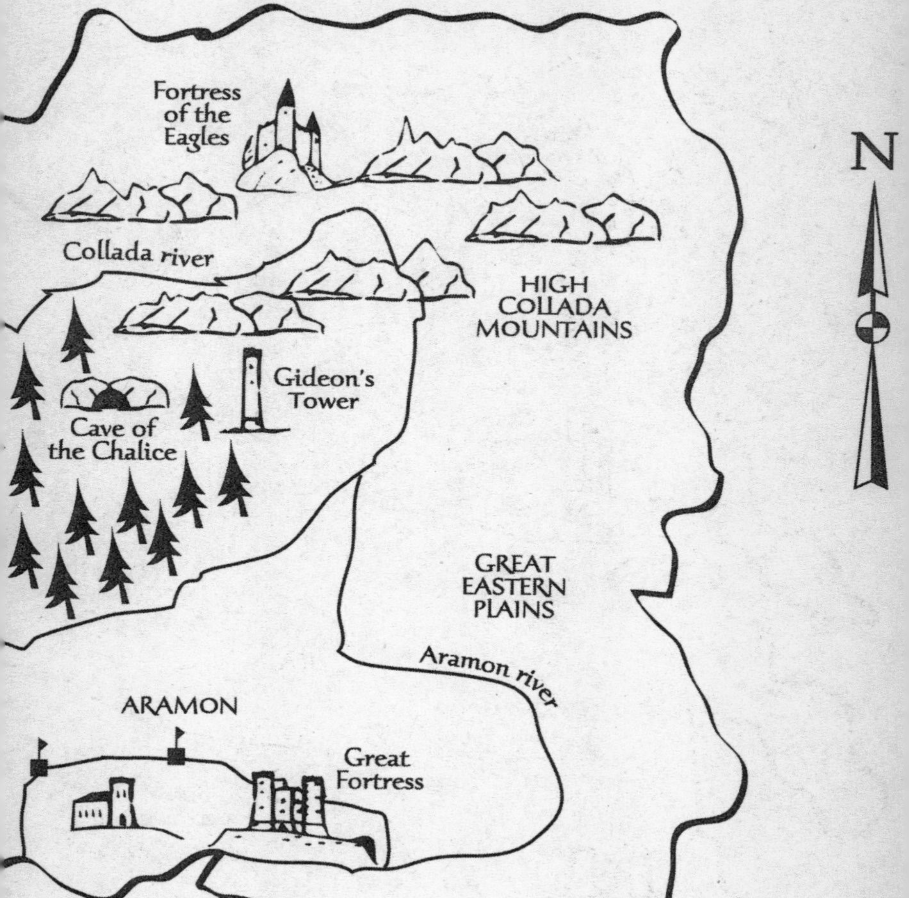

Fortress
of the
Eagles

N

Collada river

HIGH
COLLADA
MOUNTAINS

Gideon's
Tower

Cave of
the Chalice

GREAT
EASTERN
PLAINS

Aramon river

ARAMON

Great
Fortress

Part One

The Quest Begins

1 The Enchanted Crown

In the Great Hall of the Rats' Castle, a thousand warriors were feasting. Flaring torchlight glittered on jewelled daggers, and threw rippling shadows across the long tables laden with dishes and jugs of wine.

Old King Zagora sat at the high table, cramming food into his massive bulk, unaware that two rats were watching him closely.

'Why don't he let us invade the Mouse Kingdom?' grumbled Captain Gobtooth. 'The warband's never been so strong. All we have to do is cross the border. A quick campaign, an' we'd be masters of all Carminel!'

'He fears the ancient prophecy,' replied Saraband. The Warrior Chief was ruthless, ambitious, and the most feared rat in the castle. 'Surely even you know that, Gobtooth. When the mice of Carminel are in peril, a great King will arise, the dreaded eagles will fly to their aid, and we shall be driven into the sea. Naturally, I don't believe it.'

'Load of rubbish,' agreed Gobtooth. 'Where's this Mouse-King hiding, then? Here in our castle, I suppose!' He cackled with laughter. 'The eagles haven't been seen for years. Even if they did return, our Red Kites would soon see them off.' The Red Kites were not at the feast. They were on duty on the castle battlements, their cruel eyes burning into the darkness. 'Prince Karabas don't believe in prophecies,' added Gobtooth.

Saraband scowled. 'Karabas is a fool! Every day he angers King Zagora by demanding that we go to war with Carminel. He'll never learn . . .' He lowered his voice. 'We must be patient, Gobtooth. Zagora's old. He won't last for ever. Look how much he eats – and drinks! It's a wonder he doesn't burst! And when he dies, Karabas will order the war-band to march against Carminel!'

The slave-mice who overheard him turned away to hide their bitter despair. Ragged, half starved, each wore an iron collar – the mark of slavery.

The feast was held every year to celebrate the long-ago Battle of Collada River. An invading force of rats and Red Kites had defeated the Mouse-King, and sent his allies, the great eagles, flying back to the High Collada Mountains. But, in spite of their victory, the rats had lost many warriors. A peace treaty was signed. The rats kept their prisoners as slaves, and took the land between Carminel and the sea. King Zagora left the Mouse-Kingdom in peace. But if Karabas became King . . .

In the gallery that encircled the Hall, where the torchlight darkened to black, oily smoke, one slave-mouse was hiding in the shadows. His black fur had a curious reddish tinge. His name was Rufus. Many years ago his father had led an uprising of slaves. He had paid for its failure with his life. Shortly afterwards, Rufus's gentle mother had died of a broken heart. In Rufus, the flame of rebellion burnt. He longed for vengeance – and freedom!

Every year, on the stroke of midnight, King Zagora ordered the slaves to leave the hall. What happened next, Rufus was determined to find out. If the rats spotted him, he would be killed.

The castle clock struck twelve. As the rats scraped their plates clean, and drained the last of their wine, Zagora drew his sword and banged it on the table for silence. 'All slaves to the kitchen!'

Rufus tensed. As the mice filed out, the rats moved to the sides of the Hall. One by one the torches were put out, until only three were burning. King Zagora's massive body was quivering; Prince Karabas's eyes were nearly popping out of his head. Several warriors nervously shuffled their feet. Only Saraband stood motionless, a quiet smile on his face. At the far end of the Hall, a door was flung open – and Rufus had to bite his tongue to force back a cry of terror.

Out of the darkness came a creature from a nightmare, lurching forward on triple-pronged talons, huge wings folded at its sides. Sleek feathers crowned its head, and eyes burnt on either side of a great curving beak that ended in a point like a dagger. Another figure entered, identical to the first. As they moved together down the Hall, the great feathered cloaks sweeping down their backs, a distant memory stirred in Rufus . . . But it vanished as two more figures entered. One was Morvan, the black-robed High Priest and Magician of the Sable Lord of Darkness. He leant heavily on his staff, from which dangled the tails of long-dead rats. In front of him walked a younger priest, carrying a cushion. On it was a crown. It looked very old: tarnished and dull. But the rats cried out and fell to their knees – all except Saraband. He was staring at the crown, his eyes glittering with greed!

In a quavering voice, Morvan cried, 'Who will shed his blood tonight?'

For the space of a heartbeat, no one spoke. Then a harsh voice rang confidently through the Hall. 'I, Saraband!' Halting before the feathered creatures, the Warrior Chief held out his left paw. Morvan cried again, his voice gaining strength from the god,

> 'By the Sable Lord of Darkness
> Who rules the land and sky!
> By sacrifice of life-blood
> The rats shall never die!'

The creature's fierce beak flashed down. Blood streamed from a great gash in Saraband's paw. The rats flinched, but their war-leader calmly took a cloth from his pocket and pressed it to the wound. With a bow to the great feathered animal, Saraband swaggered back to his place to a loud yell of praise from his warriors.

One of the feathered creatures now spoke,

> 'Fight bravely for the Sable Lord!
> And if in battle you should fall,
> Your reward is never-ending
> Feasting in the god-king's Hall!'

The voice sounded muffled. Rufus realized that these creatures were rats – priests of some strange, secret cult. But the feathers, beaks and talons . . . Vague images, like the beating of shadowy wings, swirled in Rufus's mind; but as he tried to bring them into focus, they dissolved in confusion.

The High Priest was chanting again, his voice echoing through the Hall as he called upon the god.

> 'Blood has flowed, the vow's renewed,
> Each warrior pledges life and sword!
> Now send your spirit, mighty god!
> Reveal yourself, O, Sable Lord!'

A thousand voices repeated the cry. *'Reveal yourself, O, Sable Lord!'*

Silence . . . then a gentle wind sprang up from nowhere and whispered round the Hall. The long feathered cloaks stirred and rustled. The wind strengthened, grew colder, and the great wings lifted on the icy blast. The flares died but, through the sudden darkness, Rufus saw, high in the rafters, a luminous grey mist. Something was inside it, taking shape, growing larger. Rufus shrank back – and stared in horror. It was transparent, a spirit without substance, but Rufus could feel its evil power. It was shaped like a huge rat with a long, twitching snout, blazing eyes and a tail that circled the Hall. Swooping down until it was hovering just above the priests, its great claws reached out to touch the crown.

Rufus was angry with himself for feeling afraid. But his instincts were warning him not to look at this creature. He shut his eyes. In his mind he could still see the crown, only now it was gleaming, silver-bright. He could not see who was wearing it for the dazzling light that streamed from its jewels. But above it he could clearly see magnificent birds, wheeling and soaring in a blue sky, and their talons and heads were like those of the feathered creatures in the hall.

A terrible scream rang out. Rufus opened his eyes. The rat shape was writhing in agony, its eyes blazing at a great, glowing ruby which was throbbing, like a beating heart, in the front of the crown. The ruby glowed brighter, the huge rat screamed again, and vanished with a shattering roar!

Silence . . . then all hell broke loose. Zagora seemed incapable of speech, but Saraband's voice rose above the din. 'Light the torches! Take away the crown! The ceremony is over!'

As the torches flared, the priests left, taking the glowing crown with them. 'All rats will depart!' shouted Saraband. 'And will say nothing of this on pain of death!'

Suddenly, King Zagora crashed to the floor. His staring eyes saw nothing, his breath rasped in his throat.

'The King is ill!' cried Saraband. Zagora's bodyguards clustered about him; it needed four of them to carry him out. At last, the Hall seemed deserted. Only Karabas and Saraband stayed behind.

'What does it mean?' hissed Karabas. 'Why couldn't the god touch his crown? And why did it start glowing? It never has before!'

'That *thing* is not the Sable Lord!' exclaimed Saraband. 'Merely one of his Dark Angels. If the god himself were to come, his power would blast this castle out of existence. As for the crown; it is not the Sable Lord's, although we like to pretend it is. Our ancestors captured that crown at the Battle of Collada River. It is the ancient Crown of the Mouse-Kings of Carminel.'

'But –'

'Listen, Karabas. The mice of Carminel worship the Lord of Light. Our slaves have never heard of him; we make sure of that! He's not as powerful as the Sable Lord, of course –' Saraband touched the iron hilt of his dagger to ward off ill luck '– but some of his power lies in that ruby. Why it glowed tonight, I don't know. But it means no good to us. The sooner we destroy the mice of Carminel the better. Your father has fallen into a sleep from which he may never wake. *And when he dies . . .*'

From his hiding place in the gallery, Rufus had heard enough. Carminel was in terrible danger. Rufus had to get out of the castle, cross the border, and warn the mice!

The two rats had turned away, and were whispering together down the Hall. Rufus tried to stand, but his legs were cramped. He stumbled and his iron collar scraped loudly against the stone. Saraband swung round. *How much had this mouse overheard*? 'Guards! A slave in the gallery! Fifty gold pieces for the rat who catches him – and fifty lashes for those who don't!'

2 Red Kite

Rufus fled. As he pelted down the stairs he heard the guards yelling, and he sprinted down a passage, skidded round a corner and almost fell into the kitchen.

Smoke, steam, noise, and a crowd of slaves scurrying about with pots and pans. Rufus charged through them all, sending scalding soup and piles of plates cascading to the floor. Another uproar as the rats charged in, yelling as they slithered into the bubbling soup-lake and screaming as they crashed against the red-hot ovens.

Rufus was searching for a weapon. A guard, dripping with soup, forced his way through the seething crowd of slaves and grabbed Rufus's arm, but the mouse seized a heavy frying pan and lashed out. As the rat squealed and fell, Rufus grabbed the longest carving knife he could see. He leapt for the door and fled into the courtyard.

The castle's grim outer wall reared black against the night sky. In its shadow was the wide drain which carried slops and rubbish to the moat. Rufus clambered on to the edge of the drain, took a deep breath, and jumped. A rush of darkness, and he was deep below the scummy surface of the moat. He struggled wildly against the slime that was dragging him down to the weeds. Forcing himself to be calm, he reached upwards, and floated to the surface.

Fed by an underground spring, the filthy water moved sluggishly round the castle before draining into a lake. Rufus lay on his back, trying to steady his gasping breath, allowing the water to carry him along. Cries of frustration reached his ears: inside the castle, the rats had lost him. But high on the battlements hung the Red Kites. Rufus shut his eyes, hoping that from that height he would look like one of the many bits of rubbish floating on the surface.

At last, revolted by the greasy feel and sickening stench of the water, Rufus opened his eyes and saw that he was approaching the lake. Beyond that reared a dense forest. He had only to reach it . . .

Grabbing a tuft of grass, he hauled himself out – and froze. A Red Kite had seen him and was rising from its perch. Rufus drew his knife. As the shadow hovered over him, he hacked and lunged until suddenly the knife struck home. With a shriek, the bird soared into the sky. Rufus ran for the forest. As the trees loomed above him, he glanced up. The Red Kite was plummeting towards him.

Rufus forced himself to stand still. At the last second, as the great bird spread its wings and reached out its talons, the little mouse flung himself aside, sprang to his feet and lunged with all his strength. The Red Kite fell dead without a sound.

Trembling violently, Rufus dragged his knife free. But, as he glanced fearfully towards the castle, he saw a dark cloud rising above the battlements; the other Red Kites were coming for him. He turned and ran.

3 The Dark Angel

Rufus was hiding in a bramble bush. Above, the Red Kites were screeching as they circled the woods. They could not see him. But he knew of the Sable Lord's power to see into his mind and betray him to his enemies, so Rufus resolutely filled his thoughts with the picture that had come to him in the gallery: the shining crown and the majestic birds circling in the sky.

Rufus awoke with a groan, feeling cold and very hungry. It was still dark, and the forest was deathly silent. He found a stick and did his best to scrape the dried mud off his rags. Then he crawled out of the brambles and groped his way through the trees. Soon, he reckoned, he would arrive at the border that divided the Rat-Lands from the Mouse-Kingdom of Carminel. But, as every slave knew, the border was guarded by the Sable Lord's powerful magic: a deadly, invisible barrier, which Rufus would cross at his peril.

On he went until the stars began to fade. He crept cautiously from tree to tree until he found himself on the edge of a broad clearing. On the far side a wooden signpost bore a single word, just visible in the first glimmerings of dawn: Carminel.

As Rufus left the shelter of the trees, an icy wind froze his brain and turned his legs to stone. In the mist that was swirling round the clearing, something was taking shape. Something scaly, without legs or paws. A snake. But one more horrible than Rufus had ever imagined. Swiftly its body uncoiled to the height of the trees. A spiny collar reared behind its head, its eyes glittered, its jaws opened. The head was swaying, the eyes searching. Then it saw him. It plunged towards him, forked tongue flickering, green eyes blazing, and Rufus drew back his arm and hurled his knife straight at its face.

But no mortal weapon could harm the Dark Angel! As its jaws gaped wider, Rufus forced his legs to move, staggered clumsily backwards, tripped, and fell. But, as the creature's grinning head swung down, Rufus saw a brilliant star directly above him. Ever brighter it blazed until broad streams of purest light were spinning round the great snake, trapping its coils in gleaming coils of their own. The Dark Angel's head reared up, its body writhed in agony and a terrible, despairing cry rang across the clearing. Rufus shut his eyes, and heard a voice.

> 'Fear not these shadows, these dream-
>   haunting ogres:
> Show them your courage and put them to
>   flight!
> Always remember, when nightmares oppress
>   you –
> The darkness must always give way to the
>   light!'

Rufus had no idea who had spoken but, when he opened his eyes, the Dark Angel had gone, the star had faded and dawn light was creeping through the branches. He sat up. Beyond the clearing he could see open heathland; and from somewhere a long way off, a thin column of smoke was rising.

Seth the Blacksmith plunged the glowing blade into a tub of water. Steam rose as the metal hissed and turned a dull grey. Seth knew that the sword was now as hard as it would ever be. Later, he would sharpen it, then hide it with the others in his cellar. One day his swords would equip an army to drive out the hated rats for ever. He mopped his brow and was wondering whether to stop for a bite to eat when there came a faint scrabbling at his door. Seth opened it – and a ragged mouse almost collapsed on the step.

'Lord o' Light!' he exclaimed. 'A runaway slave! Come in, come in! You look half starved. Now, food first – then we'll see what's to be done for you!'

After shovelling more charcoal on to the furnace, Seth bustled about, setting the table with bread, cheese, cold pease pudding, and two mugs of home-brewed cider.

The blacksmith chewed slowly, but Rufus ate ravenously. Between mouthfuls, he astonished Seth with his story. '. . . so if Zagora dies, Saraband and Karabas will attack Carminel. I must warn someone. But I don't know who!'

'Don't worry about that,' said Seth with a grim

smile. 'I know who to warn. You'd better come with me!'

'Can you get this collar off me first? It marks me as a slave and I hate it!'

'That's easily done!' Taking a file, Seth set to work until the collar split and fell. 'Now, I'll find you some decent clothes and burn these rags . . . Hello, what's that?'

Seth was pointing to a chunk of blackened metal hanging from a chain round Rufus's neck. The mouse ducked his head to look.

'I don't know . . . I've never seen it before.'

'Well, you wouldn't. The slave-ring hid it. Till now.'

'It's a locket, I think. Perhaps you could open it.'

'Later! We've a long journey ahead of us –'

'Seth!' The door burst open and a young mouse stood panting on the step. 'Red Kites! Heading this way!'

4 The Castle in the Marshes

As the Red Kites landed, Saraband and his two followers, Nym and Skillet, flung themselves to the ground. Before them, the little cottages crouched in a circle round the village pond. The young mice, fearing another slave-raid, had pelted off into the fields. The old folk huddled round their fires, waiting helplessly for whatever the rats might do to them. They did not have long to wait.

At Saraband's command, Nym and Skillet charged

through the village like a whirlwind, ripping beds until the feathers flew, upending cupboards, poking their swords through floors and ceilings, and grabbing small valuables. Rampaging into the gardens, they hacked hen-houses to pieces. Saraband wanted the slave found. And he wanted him dead.

At last, Nym and Skillet met outside Seth's forge. 'He ain't in any of them 'ouses, sir! I swear he ain't,' said Nym.

'Then he must be in this one. Get in and find him!' Saraband shouted.

'Sir!' The rats kicked down the door and blundered in.

Saraband knew that Zagora was close to death; but if that accursed slave warned the mice about the invasion, they would have time to gather an army, and the rats' advantage of surprise would be lost.

'Sir! Look!' Skillet was running out of the forge. 'A slave-ring! The blacksmith must have taken it off him!'

'So that's where he was hiding. Where is he now?'

'Gone, sir. The place is empty. But there are tracks of two mice leading down to the valley behind the village.'

Saraband glowered at the forge. 'Burn it,' he snarled. 'Burn the whole village! Then find that mouse. The blacksmith is risking his neck for a runaway slave, and I know why! Go on foot. I don't want Red Kites flying about for every mouse within miles to see. I'm going back to the castle. The King's dying, and there's no knowing what Karabas will get up to if I'm not there.'

Nym and Skillet grinned. Like the rest of the warband, they respected Zagora but despised the foolish Prince. As the Red Kites vanished over the treetops, the two rats returned to the forge and pumped the bellows until the charcoal glowed white. Taking a shovelful each, they ran outside and hurled the charcoal on to the thatch. They watched in glee as the fire leapt from one roof to the next until the neat little cottages were smouldering ruins. After they left, the mice, who had fled in terror from beneath their blazing roofs, stared in dismay at the wreckage of their homes. In despair, they cursed the Rat-Kind and prayed to the Lord of Light to deliver them from the tyranny of Saraband.

Meanwhile, Seth was leading Rufus across field and moor. After a lifetime in the Rats' Castle, Rufus at first felt bewildered by the open spaces. But as the autumn sun warmed his fur, and his whiskers thrilled to the myriad scents of the countryside, he realized that he was free at last. He gazed in wonder at the ever-changing horizon. But, when he glanced back, he saw a distant column of smoke and guessed its meaning.

'Don't fret about it,' said Seth. 'We'll rebuild it. 'It ain't the first village the rats have burnt and it won't be the last. But we'll get our own back!'

After a long trek across open country, they descended to a thickly-wooded valley. The ground became soft, and large pools shone darkly beneath the trees. 'Follow me close!' warned Seth. 'Keep to the track. These marshes are dangerous.'

Rufus obeyed, wrinkling his snout at the smell of decay rising from the marsh. The track seemed to suck at his feet, which left little pools at every step. At last, Seth halted and Rufus saw, above the tangle of trees, the towers of a castle.

'Walk quietly now,' said Seth. 'We're almost there.'

With a whirr and a thud, an arrow flew overhead and buried itself in a tree behind them, and a voice cried, 'Stop where you are!'

Seth grinned. ' 'T is me. Seth! And I've brought a friend!'

Suddenly, all around them, figures rose from the marsh. They were mice, dressed in woodland colours and armed with homemade axes, knives and sickles. Down the track, a mouse-girl appeared, stooping beneath the branches. She was dressed like the others, but she carried a bow, and a quiver of arrows hung at her back.

'Seth! What are you doing here? And who's this?'

'His name's Rufus; he's a runaway slave.'

'*What*? Are the rats after him? Don't you realize that if they trace him to here, they might attack the castle?'

'I don't think they'll find us,' replied Seth calmly. 'In any case . . .'

'King Zagora's dying,' said Rufus. 'And when he's dead, Saraband will lead his warriors against Carminel.'

'That's nothing new,' retorted the mouse-girl. 'We're always hearing rumours of Zagora's death!'

'This isn't a rumour,' said Rufus, keeping his temper with an effort.

Seth said firmly, 'Elana – young Rufus has a story I want your father to hear. And you, too! So let us pass!'

Elana shrugged. 'Oh, very well. But don't blame

me if the rats come and kill us all!'

The mice escorted Seth and Rufus through the marsh until the trees ended and the castle stood before them. As he followed Elana across the drawbridge, Rufus looked up at the twin towers that flanked the gatehouse. From one of them, a flag was fluttering; emblazoned upon it was a star with streams of light.

Inside, the castle was a ruin. The only building left was the roofless shell of the Great Hall, the dying sunlight streaming through its empty windows. The mice who lived here had built rough shelters against the great tumbles of grey stone that littered the courtyard.

'They are all refugees,' Seth explained. 'Once they lived in villages, until the rats burnt them. So they stay in this old ruin. It's far enough from the border for the rats not to bother with it. But if Zagora dies, Saraband may attack this castle! My cellar is stuffed with weapons, and its entrance is too well hidden for the rats to find. Trouble is, there's only about fifty mice here and the rats have a thousand warriors. But we'll hold 'em off as long as we can. Now, I must go and pass on your warning. Wait here.'

The courtyard was twinkling with the light of

cooking fires. Elana appeared with a steaming bowl of potatoes, carrots and parsnips. Rufus was hungry after his long journey and his whiskers twitched in eager anticipation.

'We grow our own vegetables,' said Elana. 'I suppose in the Rats' Castle you've been living off the fat of the land.'

'The rats eat well. The slaves get slops and leftovers.'

Elana scowled. 'Oh . . . Well, I suppose I can't blame you for running away. But what's so special about you? Seth's no fool. He must have brought you here for a good reason.'

'He did!'

Rufus swung round and saw an old mouse, dressed in threadbare robes and leaning heavily on a staff tipped with a silver star.

'Father,' said Elana, 'this is Rufus. Rufus – my father, Amren. He is a priest of the Lord of Light.' As Elana guided the old mouse to a place by the fire, Rufus realized that he was blind.

'You are welcome,' the old priest said. 'I have already dictated a letter to Cardinal Odo, who rules Carminel from the city of Aramon. It is to warn him that Saraband may soon be on his way. Seth has told me of your adventures but we should all be glad to hear them from your own lips.'

The mice gathered round to listen. Even the sentries on the walls half-turned their heads, the better to hear him.

'What a miraculous escape!' exclaimed Amren as Rufus ended his story. 'It's not every mouse who sees visions of eagles, and gets rescued by the Lord of Light!'

'So they *were* eagles. My mother once told me about them. But I wonder how I saw them . . . Who is the Lord of Light?'

'The god of the Mouse-Kind,' answered Amren. 'The rats ensure that no word of him reaches their slaves – the better to keep you in fear of the Sable Lord. But the Lord of Light lives, far, far away, on the Island of Peace, and his spirit watches over us. He stands for the good that dwells in every mouse –'

'While the Sable Lord is ruthless and cruel, like the vermin who worship him,' said Elana fiercely. 'What do you think about Rufus's story, Father?'

'Have you ever heard of the Treasures of Carminel?' Amren asked Rufus. 'You saw one of them last night: the ancient Crown, which we believed was lost for ever. It bears the great ruby, which once was set in the sword-hilt of King Vygan, the first of the Mouse-Kings. How we shall rescue it from our enemies' castle, I do not know . . . But there are two other Treasures: the Chalice and the Sword.'

'Where are they?' asked Rufus.

Amren sighed. 'No mouse knows. But when they are found, the eagles which you saw in your vision will fly again, and the rats will be driven from Carminel. So says the ancient prophecy. Listen carefully: the Chalice is the cup used by the Lord of Light when he was with us, in his bodily form, long ages ago. It holds some of his power, and is a potent weapon against evil, though its main purpose is to do good.

'The Sword belonged to a mouse called Gideon, Eagle Warrior and Champion of Carminel. He died many years before the great Rat Invasion. Had he lived to lead his eagles against the attackers, the outcome might have been very different. But somewhere, his sword lies hidden, and it has great power. Gideon, it is said, once travelled to the Island of Peace, far across the ocean, and there received the blessing of the Lord of Light himself. No enemy of Carminel can stand against the Sword.

'Rufus, from all you have told us, I believe that you have been chosen by the Lord of Light to find these Treasures. And you must begin your search at once. If, as you say, Zagora is close to death, then Carminel is in deadly peril.'

'Oh, Father!' cried Elana. 'We can't be certain of that. Besides, how can Rufus possibly go looking for the Treasures? They might be anywhere! You can't expect him just to go wandering off and hope for the best.'

'I don't. Indeed, I confidently expect that Rufus will know where to search before he leaves this castle.'

Outside, Nym and Skillet were creeping to the edge of the moat. The sentries might have spotted them but they were distracted by Rufus's story. The rats positioned themselves opposite a gaping hole in the wall to listen . . .

'Rufus!' Seth was pointing at the diamond-shaped locket. While Amren had been speaking, Rufus had, unconsciously, been running his paw back and forth across the age-blackened metal. Now it was gleaming, silver bright!

'Father,' said Elana. 'Round Rufus's neck, there's a silver locket engraved with the Star of the Lord of Light! Where did you get it, Rufus?'

From the furthest corner of Rufus's memory, a picture was slowly emerging. 'My mother gave it to me before she died. I was only a child. She said I must guard it always . . . If these Treasures will help to drive out the rats, I'll find them! But I'll need some clues.' Reaching up his paws, Rufus unhooked the chain and passed the locket to Seth. 'Open it. There may be something useful inside.'

5 The Clue

'Well? What happened next?'

In the Great Hall, Saraband was listening with mounting dismay to his rats' report.

'His name's Rufus,' said Skillet. 'We heard that. Then there was this poem, hidden in the locket.'

'That's right,' said Nym. 'Quite a nice poem, though I didn't understand all of it. Poetry ain't much in my line. Now, a good story –'

'*Great Sable Lord of Darkness*!' Saraband crashed his fist on the table. 'Tell me what the poem said before I throw you to the Kites.'

Nym sighed and scratched his mangy fur. 'No way *I* could remember a poem.' But, seeing the look in Saraband's eyes, he added hastily, 'Skillet wrote it down. Show 'im, Skills.'

Skillet fished in his pocket and produced a dirty scrap of paper. Saraband snatched it, carried it to the window and read:

> In a cave by a fountain the Chalice lies hidden;
> Releasing the rainbow reveals it to sight.
> Under a fortress the Sword is concealed –
> Gideon's rapier, blessed by the Light.
> Only the god knows the fate of the Ruby;
> The past is a horror, the future a void –
> But go with the Treasures and seek for the eagles:
> The King shall arise and the rats be destroyed.

Saraband's face was a mask of horror. 'What happened next?' he whispered.

'Well, nothin',' said Skillet. 'They all started talkin' at once, then they changed the guard on the walls, so we reckoned we'd better scarper. Any case, it was gettin' late, and we 'adn't 'ad no supper –'

'Fools!' screamed Saraband. 'Get out before I tear you to pieces.'

The rats fled. 'Curse that slave!' shouted Saraband. 'He overheard everything I said to Karabas after the feast, and will no doubt have blabbed it all to that blacksmith, and to the old fool at the castle. Will he have gone after the Treasures already?' Saraband glared out at the mist. It was not usually so dense at this time of year and would hinder the search for Rufus. 'Is some enchantment already at work?'

From the room above, he could hear the chanting of the priests as they cast their spells and prayed for the King's life. Saraband sneered. It would take a miracle to cure Zagora now. And when he died – all-out war against Carminel!

But the mice must not be allowed to get their paws on those Treasures. Who knew what magic they might work? Saraband looked again at the poem. The reference to the Chalice meant nothing, but, *Under a fortress the Sword lies concealed* ... Of course! The Great Fortress of Aramon that guarded the capital of Carminel. Saraband must get there before that accursed slave. He thought of the Crown. Whoever had written the poem had not known where it was. At least Saraband had that.

The priests' chanting stopped. The castle fell silent. Suddenly the door burst open and Prince Karabas dashed in. 'He's dead! At last.'

'Excellent!' cried Saraband. 'So now you're King . . .'

'YES!' Karabas hurled himself dramatically on to his dead father's throne. 'We must hold the coronation at once; the warriors will expect it! And I must have a new robe. Purple velvet with gold trimmings – or should it be gold velvet with –'

Saraband stopped listening. You pathetic fool, he thought; the Sable Lord has got rid of your father. Now I must get rid of you. Accidents often happen in a war . . . a bullet in the back – a dagger between the shoulders. Then my warriors will surely acclaim me as King.

Karabas was prattling on. '. . . and I shall expect a really expensive coronation present.'

Saraband smiled. 'What does your majesty desire most in all the world?'

Karabas looked blank; then he whispered, 'War! War against the Mouse-Kind.'

'Exactly. So let the priests bury your father, and you can have your coronation in Aramon.'

Leaving Karabas to his dreams of glory, Saraband hurried off. After giving orders to his warriors, he went to see Kei, the Chief Raven, in his nest high in the North Tower. Saraband despised the ravens. The rats used them as scouts and messengers, but they were vicious and disobedient, and their filthy nests stank.

'What do you want?' mumbled Kei, his beak full of worms. 'I'm 'avin' dinner.'

'Listen, you stinking wretch, tomorrow we begin the march on Aramon. I want one flight of twelve ravens to scout ahead, and two wide-patrols, one on either flank. They're to look for a mouse with reddish-black fur. He may be alone, or he may have company. I want him found. Understood?'

'Why?'

'None of your business. But I want him dead.'

Kei fluffed up his feathers. 'Like that, is it? Yeah, well, we'll try. Can't promise nothin'. But Aramon . . . Long flight. Very tirin' . . .' He gave Saraband a sidelong glance. 'Wot's in it for us?'

'Jewels from the Cathedral and cash from the merchant-mice. Satisfied?'

'Mmm . . . S'pose so. All right. I'll tell the lads.'

'Do that. And don't oversleep or I'll feed you to the Kites. We march at dawn.'

6 Mice Beware!

'Listen!'

Crouching beneath the low-hanging branches of a willow, Elana peered into the mist. She had heard something, and now Rufus caught it too: the muffled sound of tramping feet, rapidly approaching. The mice lay flat. Moisture dripped from the tree and trickled down their necks. The sound grew louder until it seemed that it would swamp them. Suddenly, out of the veil of mist, burst the Rat Army.

Rank after rank they came, swinging along the valley, only yards below the tree where the mice lay hidden. Rufus was accustomed to the rats' smell, but Elana wrinkled her snout in disgust as their stench swept over her. As they swaggered by, the warriors burst into song.

> 'We're marching to Aramon – mice beware!
> We'll hack off your tails and singe your hair!
> Wherever you hide yourselves, we'll be
>   there –
> With daggers and swords all go-ry!
> Oh, our teeth are sharp, our claws are red,
> Before you can see us, you'll be dead!
> So quiver and shiver and shake with dread
> At Saraband's army in glo-ry!'

Ahead of the army, robed in cloaks patterned with silver moons, capered the priests of the Sable Lord, brandishing their staffs and muttering spells to ward off danger. Behind them hobbled old Morvan. Saraband was cloaked and helmeted for war. Karabas strutted haughtily, his breastplate gleaming under a purple cloak, a jewelled crown on his head.

A flight of shadows swooped through the mist: the Red Kites. And, invisible on the flanks of the army, the ravens were searching for Rufus.

'They're going to attack Aramon,' whispered

Elana, as the sound of tramping feet faded into the mist. 'Zagora must be dead. You were right, Rufus. Karabas was wearing a crown. Was it the Crown of Carminel?'

'No. That is either at the castle, or Saraband has it with him. Come on, the sooner we find the other Treasures the better. Let's make the most of this mist. Once it lifts, we must hide somewhere until dark. It won't be safe to travel in daylight; you can bet Saraband's got his filthy ravens looking for us.'

Rufus had no idea of their direction, but Elana seemed to know her way by instinct. Rufus was thankful that she had joined him on the quest. Elana had a sharp tongue but she would make a useful companion. For a while they walked in silence. Then Rufus asked, 'Why does a Cardinal rule in Aramon? Isn't there a King?'

'No. When the last King was old, the rats invaded. The King's only son was killed in the Battle of Collada River, so the royal line died out. Since then, Carminel has been ruled by Cardinals of the Lord of Light. The one in charge now is called Odo.'

'And when the rats attack, will he fight?'

Elana grinned. 'Not all priests are gentle, like my father. I've heard Odo keeps a wooden club to fight with.'

'Why not a sword or pistol?'

'Well, being a Cardinal, he's not supposed to shed blood, so he has his club instead, to bash rats!'

Suddenly Rufus realized that the mist was lifting. He glanced over his shoulder. 'We must find somewhere to hide – look!' Far to the south, dark specks were flying towards them. They were too far to be certain, but Rufus felt sure that they were Saraband's ravens.

Amren had told them to seek the Chalice first. 'When the Lord of Light lived in Carminel, many ages ago, he dwelt in a cave, and mice would travel from far and near to hear his message of peace. He baked his own bread, which he called the bread of life; and when he passed round the Chalice, filled with his own blackberry wine, it never ran dry, no matter how many mice had drunk from it. He called the wine the symbol of brotherhood. According to Rufus's poem, the Chalice is still in the cave. If you follow the old Pilgrims' Way, you should find it.'

First though, they had to find the Pilgrims' Way. They journeyed by night, sleeping by day in dry ditches or deep in the woods. When their food ran out, Elana introduced Rufus to blackberries, elderberries, and sloes, which the country-mice called wild plums.

As they journeyed further from Saraband's line of march, they judged it safe to travel by day. The country-mice were bringing in the last of the harvest. They shared their bread, cheese and rough cider with Rufus and Elana, and at night welcomed them to their farmsteads. Clouds of black smoke on the southern horizon told a grim tale of farms and fields put to the torch, so the country-mice lived in terror of the invaders. Rufus longed to cheer them by telling of their quest for the Treasures, but he dared not, lest Saraband should hear of it.

Leaving the rich farmlands, Rufus and Elana descended to a densely wooded valley. By Elana's reckoning, they were not very far from where the Chalice of the Lord of Light was hidden. 'This must be the old Pilgrims' Way,' she said, as they set off along a narrow track. 'According to my father's directions, we should be getting near to the cave.'

All that morning, Rufus and Elana struggled to follow the path. Just when they thought it lost, it would reappear, leading them deeper and deeper into the forest. At midday they stopped. While Elana foraged for hazelnuts and hawthorn berries, Rufus rested, watching the pattern of dappled sunlight beneath the trees . . . Suddenly, a shadow rippled across the path. Rufus glanced up. A raven was flying above the wood. As it dipped below the tree-tops, Rufus darted across the path and dived under a holly bush. 'Elana!' he called. There was no reply.

But Elana had spotted the raven. As it swooped overhead, she unslung her bow, fitted an arrow and waited. When the raven, flying lower this time, made a second circuit of the woods and was directly above her, she raised her bow, took a split-second aim, and fired.

Rufus emerged from his hiding place to see Elana grimly retrieving her arrow from the dead bird. 'We must bury it quickly,' she said, 'and then get moving. Luckily, this spy was alone. I don't think I could have dealt with more than one.'

Elana was wrong. The raven's partner, Kei, flying towards the wood, had veered sharply at the sight of his friend's death, and flown back to the army.

'You never said this 'ere mouse 'ad a bow an' arrows,' Kei said accusingly.

'How was I to know?' retorted Saraband. 'And stop whining. You're paid well for your scouting and you know the risks. Your friend should have been more careful. Nym! Skillet! Mount up! Find that slave! He's probably going for the Chalice. Find out where it's hidden, then kill him and whoever's with him. Kei will guide you. Oh, yes you will,' he snarled, as the disgruntled raven began sidling away. 'If you don't want to end up as Kite fodder.'

7 Mould-Warp

'They're not just behind us,' whispered Rufus. 'They're all around!'

'There's someone behind, and someone approaching from in front,' murmured Elana. Her bow was ready, arrowhead gleaming in the darkness. 'And there are others, keeping pace with us on either side. You're right, we're surrounded.'

Rufus gripped his dagger. At least this fight would be against living enemies, not Dark Angels who still came at night and haunted his dreams.

'Rufus!'

Nym and Skillet suddenly appeared. Elana drew her bow and fired at Skillet. Rufus snarled and flung himself at Nym. The rat was strong, but Rufus gripped Nym's throat with his right paw, kicked his feet from under him, and hurled him to the ground. Sitting astride, he gripped Nym's neck with both paws, but Nym's feet came up and threw Rufus off. He landed on his feet and, as Nym struggled to get up, Rufus launched himself in a vicious head-butt. As Nym fell, Rufus drew his dagger . . . And froze.

Elana's arrow had missed. Skillet had seized her and stuffed a filthy rag into her mouth. His pistol was pointing at her head. Nym staggered up, rubbing his aching neck. He helped himself to Rufus's dagger. 'Saraband wants to know where this 'ere Chalice is,' he panted. 'So tell us.'

How did Saraband know? 'I'll tell you,' Rufus replied. 'But first let her go.'

'Just tell us,' said Skillet. 'Then we'll see. Who knows? We might let both of you go.'

'Don't lie. You've been sent to kill me. But you've no reason to kill her.'

'Oh, no?' sneered Skillet. 'Who shot that poxy raven, then? You're right, we are goin' to kill you, you snivelling wretch, but tell us where this Chalice-thing is, and we might let her go.'

Elana's eyes held a clear command: say nothing! But Rufus ignored her. So long as there was a chance of saving her, he would tell these rats all he knew. 'The Chalice –'

'NO!' A roar from the woods and huge shadows rose from the ground on either side of the path.

'RATS! Throw your guns to the ground!'

Nym and Skillet glanced at one another, hurled the mice aside, raised their pistols, and – 'AAAAAARRRGGGHHH!'

Two axes had flickered out of the shadows, the pistols had skittered into the bushes and the rats were hopping about the path, clutching their paws where the axes had bitten deeply.

'Now go!' ordered the voice. 'We shall not kill you this time. But if you or any of your kind venture here again, you will not leave this wood alive. Return to your Red Kites. You will be watched every step of the way, although you will not see who watches you. Now GO!'

The rats fled. Elana tore the gag from her mouth, grabbing her water flask to rinse away the vile taste. Rufus watched warily as the shadows approached.

The strangers stood taller than the mice, and were armed with axes, knives, pistols and ancient flintlocks. But their best weapons, Rufus noticed, were their huge forepaws, one of which their leader now raised solemnly in greeting.

'I am Rothgar. We are the Mould-Warp,' he announced in a deep rumble. 'In our ancient language, it means earth-turners. But you may know of us as Moles.'

'I have heard of you,' said Elana, 'and I have heard that you are friends of the Mouse-Kind. Thank you for –'

'We are nothing of the sort!' exclaimed another mole. 'To my way of thinking, you are not much better than the rats. All we ask is to be left alone. If I were Lord Rothgar, I'd have killed those other vermin and you too.'

'But you are not me, Oslaf,' replied the first mole. 'And as long as I lead the war-band, you will obey my orders.' He turned to the mice. 'I am indeed a friend of the Mouse-Kind, and would allow you to continue your journey. But our Queen, Morganna, wishes to see you. No harm will befall you,' he added, with a warning glance at Oslaf. 'Please come with me. Now.'

Rufus resented being ordered about. 'What if we refuse?'

'I am under orders,' replied Rothgar quietly. 'Please do not make me use force – and don't give Oslaf an excuse to kill you.'

Rufus wanted to go on with the quest. Every day, the rats were drawing nearer to Aramon. Rothgar, he sensed, was honourable, but Oslaf was a dangerous enemy.

'Oh, let's go with the moles,' said Elana. 'Just for one night. We'll have somewhere to sleep. I'm tired.'

Perhaps Elana was right. Tomorrow they would be on their way again. 'All right.'

As they followed Rothgar deeper into the woods, dark clouds rolled across the sky, lightning flickered above the treetops and thunder rumbled menacingly in the distance.

8 Rhiannon

The huge underground chamber was dimly lit with rushlights. At the far end sat a small mole. An embroidered robe hung from her shoulders, a circle of gold gleamed on her head, and a pair of spectacles was perched on her snout. She was flanked by the solemn-looking members of the Royal Council.

Queen Morganna seemed a curiously lonely figure, Elana thought. Her brow was furrowed with care and her eyes, though kindly, looked clouded, as if she were deeply troubled. But she listened politely as Rothgar introduced the mice and explained their presence in the wood.

'So, you are after Treasure. How exciting. What did Rothgar say it was?'

'A Chalice, your Majesty,' said Rufus, 'which the Mouse-Kind need in order to defeat the rats, who are even now marching on Aramon.'

'Do you know where to look?' asked the Queen.

'Well . . . yes.'

The Queen smiled. 'You don't sound very certain! Rest here tonight as our guests. In the morning, Lord Rothgar and some of his warriors will escort you through the woods, and help you in your quest.'

'And when you have found the Chalice, bring it back so that we can all admire it!' A beautiful young mole, wearing a silver coronet, had swept into the chamber. She took her seat next to the Queen, and stared haughtily at the mice.

'I see no reason for that,' said Morganna coldly. 'I doubt whether this Treasure will be of any interest to us; and these young mice have a war to fight.'

Oslaf said, 'If the Princess Rhiannon wishes to see the Treasure, surely she should be allowed to? I should like to see it too!'

Several of the Councillors were muttering agreement. The Queen frowned. 'Oh, very well. If my sister is so eager to see it. Lord Rothgar, will you escort our guests back from their quest and satisfy the Princess Rhiannon's curiosity?'

Rothgar bowed, but shot a venomous look at Oslaf and Rhiannon. Rufus caught the greedy glint in the Princess's eyes. If she once got her paws on the Chalice, she might be most unwilling to let it go! Still, the old Queen seemed friendly enough.

'She's a bit vague, though,' said Elana, as they lay uncomfortably on the earthen floor of their sleeping-chamber. 'Rothgar seems all right. But did you see the way Oslaf and Rhiannon were smiling at each other? And the way some of those Councillors pricked up their ears at the mention of Treasure? Can we give them the slip?'

'Not tonight. We'd never find our way out of this maze of tunnels. As for tomorrow, I've heard that in daylight moles are practically blind.'

'But they can hear and smell much better than we can. And we've seen how quickly they react to danger.'

'I'm sure we can move faster and escape,' said Rufus.

But next morning, back on the Pilgrims' Way, the mice found themselves neatly boxed in by six well-armed warriors, with Rothgar in the lead. 'Just tell me when to stop,' he called over his shoulder as they set off. The other moles said nothing. Their eyes were almost invisible, their faces without expression.

Rufus felt angry. What sort of treatment was this? Did the moles want the Chalice?

After a while, the path began to climb between a tumble of boulders, and there were fewer trees. Suddenly Rothgar stopped. 'I can hear running water. Didn't you say you were looking for a fountain?'

'Yes!' exclaimed Rufus. 'But I can't see one.'

Rothgar hastened up the track, his quivering ears picking up sounds inaudible to the mice. He led them off the path to a little grove of trees, where a spring was bubbling between boulders. Behind it, the grassy rock-strewn slope rose steeply to a tree-lined ridge. The air was very still. The light was almost dazzling.

'Here is your water,' said Rothgar. 'But I do not sense a cave.'

'The poem said we had to release a rainbow,' said Elana. 'But I don't see how.'

'It also mentioned a fountain,' said Rufus, 'not a pathetic little trickle. Let's have a closer look.'

One of the warriors made to stop him but at Rothgar's stern command, he let him go. Rufus climbed the slope to where the water was seeping rapidly from a pile of small boulders. He guessed there was plenty of pressure there, and wondered what would happen if he cleared away some rocks. He did so and the spring bubbled higher. Delving into the spring, Rufus removed another rock, and another. Now the water was leaping higher than his head. He reached down and, with an effort, lifted out one more rock, feeling the power of the spring surge beneath his paws. As the rock came out, Rufus was thrown on to his back. A mighty jet of water shot as high as the treetops, before cascading in a sparkling curtain that glowed with colour.

Elana clapped her paws, squeaking with delight. Rothgar smiled. 'Is that your rainbow? But listen! Surely you can hear it?'

At first the mice heard nothing but the splash of water. Then, gradually, soft music of an unearthly beauty stole upon them from the heart of the rainbow. Mice and moles listened, spellbound. As the music faded, they saw that a deep shadow had appeared in the hillside.

Rufus gasped. 'Elana! It must be the opening of the cave!'

'You'd better go and see.'

Rufus took her paw, but she gently pulled away. 'No, Rufus. This is your quest. You must go alone.'

9 The Chalice

The cave was cold and dark. Rufus was wet through after his struggle with the spring, and shivered as he groped along the rock wall. At last, he sensed a vast emptiness. He glanced back, but the cave was pitch dark. He hated enclosed spaces, and breathed deeply in an effort to stem the rising tide of panic. 'Lord of Light! Show me the way!'

A faint glow, that seemed to come from the very heart of the darkness, gradually intensified. In the dim light, a mouse appeared. He was holding a plain wooden bowl. Soft light streamed from a star above his head. Gradually, shadowy figures loomed out of the darkness, all bathed in the star's gentle radiance. More mice. As Rufus watched, the mouse at the centre of the cavern raised the bowl, and drank. Then he gave it to the mouse nearest to him. As the bowl was passed round, Rufus heard a strong, clear voice: 'Drink, all of you! This wine is the symbol of brotherhood.'

Rufus stifled a gasp. It was the same voice he had heard on the night of his escape from the Rats' Castle.

At last, the bowl came to Rufus. But, as he reached for it, another mouse took it, drank from it, and passed it on. Rufus realized that he was watching a scene from the past. He kept his eyes on the Chalice, which at last returned to the mouse who had first drunk from it: the Lord of Light himself.

The mouse drank once more, then held out the bowl for all to see. It was empty. He turned, and placed it on a ledge at the far end of the cavern. As he did so, the starlight faded, and Rufus was alone in the dark.

He walked towards the invisible ledge, reached up, and his paw closed on the Chalice. Immediately he felt a tingling, as if the Chalice were filled with pent-up energy. Suddenly the cavern walls were sparkling with tiny pinpoints of light. At the far end, a glittering arch marked his way out. Clutching the precious Chalice, Rufus crossed the cavern but, as he reached the arch, he turned and looked back to where the Lord of Light had stood.

'I will keep this Chalice safe,' he promised, 'and use it to free Carminel from its enemies.'

Gradually the lights faded, until only one remained, high in the roof. The familiar voice spoke again.

'The Chalice is yours, but the quest is not
   over.
Seek for the Treasures still to be found.
And when you have won them –
   summon the eagles.
But keep up your courage, for perils abound!'

Triumphantly, Rufus ran out of the cave . . . And stopped abruptly. Elana was bound and gagged and held fast by two moles. Six others were barring his way. Cold fury swept over him. He and Elana had been betrayed after all! He was outnumbered, but at least he had the advantage of the downward slope. Setting down the Chalice, he drew his dagger and charged.

The moles had not expected this. Rufus crashed into them, lunging with his dagger, kicking viciously. A space opened up, but the other moles were moving to cut him off. He feinted left, then swung right, crashing against a mole who staggered and fell. Now only two were in front of him, and the moles holding Elana were watching him nervously. As the two advanced against him, Rufus charged them, hurling them to the ground. Elana was just in front of him, he had only her two guards to deal with but two others had closed in behind him, and they fell upon him, forcing the breath from his body. He gasped in pain as they hauled him upright, but still he struggled, lashing out with his foot. The moles squealed, but held on.

A big mole came lumbering out of the trees. 'Rothgar!' yelled Rufus. But it was Oslaf. Unable to move, Rufus stared in horror at the blood on Oslaf's axe as the big mole strode towards him.

Part Two

Aramon in Peril

10 The Cardinal

At the heart of the Great Fortress of Aramon was a pleasant garden, where a big grey mouse was sitting at a wooden table, tucking in to a gargantuan breakfast. His bowlful of cream-drenched nuts, raisins and barleycorn had already vanished into his cavernous stomach. He was just reaching for a steaming dish of eggs, mushrooms and golden-fried bread, when a black-clothed, elderly mouse, with ink-stained paws, tottered into the garden. He regarded the big grey mouse coldly through thick spectacles.

'Still shovelling that fatty food into yer poor, long-suffering innards, I see.' The clipped accent of the north-west of Carminel was frosty with disapproval, but the grey mouse smiled, and forked another mushroom.

'Won't you join me, McCrumb? There's plenty for two.'

McCrumb reeled in horror. 'I'd no' insult ma' guts wi' that greasy garbage. *When* I've time for a bit o' breakfast, it'll be a wholesome crust and a wee bowl o' porridge sprinkled with salt.'

The big mouse pulled a face. 'Sounds disgusting. Still, you'll be in good training for when the rats arrive.'

McCrumb chuckled and rubbed his inky paws. 'Aye! All food will be strictly rationed. No more greasy breakfasts for you.'

'That's true.' The grey mouse sighed at the thought, then attacked another piece of fried bread. As he munched contentedly, a little swallow circled the garden, then landed on the table. A scroll of paper was tied to her leg.

The swallow made a graceful bow, for the big grey mouse was none other than Cardinal Odo, ruler of Carminel. McCrumb, who was the Cardinal's secretary, untied the scroll, glanced at its contents, and gave a low whistle of surprise. 'Ye'd better read this yerself.'

'Another letter from my dear friend Amren at the Castle in the Marshes. Thanks to his timely warning, we are prepared for the rats.' Odo turned to the swallow. 'You have flown far, little one. Come, some eggy bread and a dish of cream to be going on with –' McCrumb tutted in disapproval. Odo ignored him '– then forage in the garden for earwigs and worms.'

Cardinal Odo buttered a doorstep of toast, but as he read his letter, he forgot his breakfast. 'What amazing news. An escaped slave and Amren's daughter on a quest for the Treasures. The slave, Rufus, had the clues in his mother's locket. Hmmm – there's more to this than meets the eye. But if they find the Treasures, and the eagles, you realize what this could mean?'

McCrumb nodded thoughtfully. He was learnèd in the history and legends of Carminel, and knew the ancient prophecy. 'Aye – it could mean the return of the long-lost King. Would you want that?'

'I most certainly would. Carminel needs a King. And I should like to retire to a little cottage in the country. But how much time do our Treasure-seekers have? What news of Saraband?'

McCrumb smiled sourly. 'The very worst. His advance continues unchecked. Every day, more country-mice flock to the city wi' terrible tales o' burning an' slaughter. Saraband an' his army of vermin cannot be far.'

'Well, we must just hope that Rufus and Elana find the Treasures and manage to reach the eagles in time to save us all from Saraband. But I doubt they'll manage it . . . What news of Captain Finn?'

McCrumb scowled. 'None at all! Though no doubt he an' his gang of cut-throats are out there somewhere. If any mouse can hold up Saraband's advance, it'll be Finn. A rogue and a rascal – but a grand fighter. Will ye write a reply to Amren yerself? Then, if ye'll excuse me, I've work to do.'

The Cardinal smiled, thinking of what Finn was probably up to, out there in the hills, behind the enemy's line of advance. Then his thoughts returned to Rufus. I wonder what he looks like? Poor Amren could not tell me, of course, though he has faith in him. But Rufus and Elana will have to hurry – *time is running out*!

11 The Valley of Death

'Oh, we've scoffed all their grub an' we've
    swilled their beer,
We've looted and plundered from far and
    near,
We'll soon be in Aramon, never fear!
We're Saraband's army in glo-ry!'

Plundering, burning, the great army swept across
Carminel, the terrified country-mice fleeing before
it. The rats seized as much food as they could carry
before leaving farmhouses and fields in flames.

At last, only one obstacle lay between the rats and Aramon: a region of thickly-wooded hills. Leaving the open country behind them, the warriors entered a maze of narrow, twisting valleys with steep sides vanishing into shrouds of mist. The army sang no longer, but marched in watchful silence. It was obvious, even to the most confident rat, that this was the perfect place for an ambush; and Nym and Skillet were feeling far from confident.

Furious over their dismal failure to kill Rufus, Saraband had banished them from the Flying Cavalry and put them with the vanguard of the infantry, the place of greatest danger. Their new commander, the savage Captain Gobtooth, made the two rats' lives a misery with his constant jeers and sarcastic remarks.

'Scarpered from a bunch of flea-ridden muck-shovellers, did you? Well, now you can join the foot-sloggers and see some real soldiering, an' if you ain't up to it, I'll soon whip you into shape!' And he had.

'Oh, my back!' groaned Nym as they trudged along the valley.

'Shut up moaning,' muttered Skillet. 'If old Gobtooth hears you, he'll give you another flogging.'

'It ain't fair!' hissed Nym. 'Everyone nods off for a few minutes on sentry duty. He's just got it in for me.'

'A few minutes, yes, not the whole flippin' night.'

'Vanguard – halt!' Gobtooth's harsh voice echoed down the track.

'Phew, that's a relief,' said Nym as they flopped to the ground. 'My feet are killing me.'

'You two!' Gobtooth was striding towards them. 'On your feet, you horrible little rats! I've got a job for you!'

With sinking hearts, Nym and Skillet trailed after him to the head of the column, trying to ignore the other rats' sneers. 'Now then,' said Gobtooth. 'See where the valley curves away out of sight? I want to know what's round that corner – and you're going to find out. The rest of the army's not far behind us, so you've got about ten minutes. Get going!'

Nym and Skillet crept forward. 'Move!' hissed Gobtooth, and the two rats broke unwillingly into a trot. But as they reached the bend in the track, they slowed down. Cautiously, they inched round the corner. At this point, a bridge carried the path over a fast-flowing stream that tumbled down the hillside and plunged into a narrow gorge leading away from the main valley. The rats crept across the bridge. Beyond, the track was deserted. No sound broke the silence.

'Phew! Let's get back,' said Nym.

'No, wait,' said Skillet. 'What's that – down the end of the track?'

'That? I dunno. A fallen tree?'

'Might be a barricade. Could be the enemy.'

'What enemy? We ain't seen a sign of the enemy!'

'Well, this might be it, you nerk! Come on, we'll tell old Gobguts, let him work it out.'

'It might be a barricade,' said the captain thoughtfully when they had made their report. 'Nym, go back to Lord Saraband. Ask him to send a couple of ravens up here.'

By the time Kei and his partner returned from their flight down the valley, Saraband had joined Gobtooth at the head of the column.

'A fallen tree,' said Kei scornfully, 'and not a mouse in sight. Honestly, if you're goin' to bother us for every little –'

'Shut up!' snapped Saraband. 'Gobtooth – march on, but keep your eyes peeled. Once the army's clear of this valley, we'll find somewhere to camp for the night. I'm going back to the main force.'

In the gathering dusk, the army advanced along the track. The valley was deathly silent. By the time the vanguard was approaching the fallen tree, the rest of the army had reached the bend in the track and was just crossing the bridge, when three things happened at once.

Gobtooth and the rats following him yelled in panic as the ground opened beneath them. They fell into a deep pit, landing painfully on a bed of brambles. At the same moment, the bridge collapsed with a deafening explosion, tipping the rats who were crossing it into the stream and cutting off the rearguard, who flung themselves flat as volleys of rifle fire crashed from the woods above.

Nym and Skillet had narrowly avoided the trap, and were bolting in terror down the path. Suddenly, from the crest of the ridge, came a strange whooshing sound. The rats looked up. Trails of light were arching into the sky. As they plummeted to earth, a series of explosions roared down the track.

'Retreat!' yelled Saraband. As the bullets zinged about them, the rats pelted back, slithering down the slopes of the gorge beneath the wrecked bridge, many yelling in terror as the fast-flowing torrent swept them away.

'Red Kites!' screamed Saraband. But as another flight of rockets soared into the air, the birds panicked and flew off to the shelter of the trees, where they perched, quivering with fright. Saraband was grinding his teeth and lashing his tail in fury. In a matter of minutes, his army was in headlong retreat. The warriors were firing at the hillside, but they could not see their enemy whose bullets, flying thick and fast, were shredding their ranks. By the time they were out of that hellish valley, the rats had suffered serious losses, several Red Kites had vanished and the army's confidence was badly shaken.

Captain Gobtooth had clambered painfully out of the pit, furious with Nym and Skillet for deserting him. 'The mice must have an army after all,' he said grimly to Saraband, as the warriors assembled on open ground once more.

'But where are they?' squeaked Karabas furiously. He had narrowly escaped a ducking in the stream, and was trying to scrape the mud from his fine cloak. 'I blame you, Lord Saraband! You'll have to improve your tactics.'

Saraband glared at him. His paws were itching to close round that conceited fool's throat! But for once, thought Saraband, the stupid Prince was right:

they were up against a remarkably cunning, and invisible, enemy. But if Saraband could have seen the mice who had ambushed him as they slipped away to their cave in the hills, he would have been astonished. The attack had been planned and carried out by just twenty-one mice: Captain Finn's elite Special Operations Unit, otherwise known as the 'Dirty Squad'.

The rat-warriors were grimly silent. At Saraband's insistence they had marched all the previous night to make up for lost time. Karabas had protested but Saraband had yelled that *he* commanded the army, not Karabas, and Karabas had been too scared to argue. The Red Kites flew continuous patrols, but Kei and his ravens had been grounded for failing to spot the hidden mice. Sulky and footsore, the birds waddled along in the wake of the army, muttering about the unfairness of life.

The rats were advancing across open moorland. Not daring to risk another ambush, Saraband had decided to make a long detour, well to the south of the hills, so that the rats would be able to see their enemy. Or so they thought.

12 The Dirty Squad

Brains cautiously raised his head. The rats were a long way off but he could still smell their lingering stench. He glanced round at his section. 'Come on!' His four mice, invisible in their green-and-brown camouflage, followed him to the next patch of cover, a shallow dip in the ground some distance ahead.

Behind them, Dead-Eye's section saw them move, and the mice followed their one-eyed leader to the spreading gorse patch just vacated by Brains's section.

Over to their right, Burglar's section was wading

up a shallow stream, hidden by high banks. Far ahead, Silence, dumb from birth but gifted with wonderful sight and hearing, directed his mice through a long swathe of tall heather, so cunningly that their movement resembled the rippling of the wind. The rats, who were almost within touching distance, failed to spot them.

Captain Finn's Dirty Squad travelled light, except for Brains's section, whose packs were stuffed with their leader's invention: the deadly exploding rockets that had so panicked the rats the day before. The Squad was armed with rapid-firing rifles, better than anything the rats had, and long, curved daggers. They were fierce gutter-fighters, recruited from the back alleys of Aramon by a leader who was every bit as tough and resourceful as the mice he commanded.

That night, even Saraband had to call a halt. The warriors collapsed and slept. Most of the sentries fell asleep at their posts and those who stayed awake failed to spot the Dirty Squad, who crept as close to the enemy as they dared. Finding a saucer-shaped dip in the ground, the mice rested, while the section leaders lay along the low ridge, watching the sleeping rats.

'Where's the Boss?' murmured Dead-Eye.

'Said he were goin' to listen in on the rats' plans,' replied Brains. 'But he should've been back by now.'

'Can you 'ear anyfink, Silence?' asked Burglar.

Silence shook his head. He felt worried; the Boss had been gone a long time.

'Why'd Saraband make 'em march so long wivout a break?' whispered Burglar. 'Wot's the 'urry? They ain't that far from Aramon now.'

'Dunno,' said Brains. 'Maybe the Boss'll find out.'

'I did!'

'Blimey, Boss!' hissed Dead-Eye. 'I never 'eard you comin'.'

'He come up-wind,' murmured Brains. 'Nice one, Boss!'

Finn smiled and stretched his long limbs, which felt cramped after his crawl through the heather. His father had been a soldier, and his father before him, right back to Conal, who had been second-in-command to the legendary Gideon, Eagle Warrior. Finn lived for the day when those eagles would fly again and drive the rats from Carminel for ever.

'Any luck, Boss?' asked Burglar.

'Yes! I know why Saraband's been rushin' along like there's no tomorrow. Tell me, did it ever occur to you to wonder how he's goin' to attack Aramon *without siege guns*?'

The mice shook their heads. Even Brains had not thought of that.

'I managed to crawl to within a few yards of Saraband and that popinjay, Karabas. They were discussin' Abbot's Cove.'

'The fishin' village?' asked Dead-Eye.

'Yes. Below the headland where the old Monastery of the Grey Mice lies in ruins. Just down the coast from Aramon. Seems they have to be there by dawn tomorrow – because that's when the ships carryin' the siege guns will be arrivin'. Saraband couldn't drag them across country, so he's had 'em brought round by sea.'

'Crafty devil,' murmured Burglar. 'So what do we do? Wait till the guns come ashore, then nick 'em?'

'Nah,' said Dead-Eye. 'Not even you could nick a load of siege guns! I say we blow 'em up.'

'We ain't got enough explosive for that,' said Brains. 'And my rockets ain't accurate enough, even if I could get close enough to fire 'em.'

Silence rhythmically waggled his paws, and blew on them to indicate ships at sea; then he pointed east, to where Aramon lay beyond the horizon.

Finn smiled. 'You've got it, Silence. There are three war galleons in the harbour at Aramon. They'll have to intercept Saraband's ships and destroy them.'

'How many ships has he got?' asked Brains.

'I don't know. Anyway, it's our only chance. Dead-Eye, take your section now, and get to Aramon fast. See the Cardinal and tell him what's happenin'. He'll do the rest – I hope!'

As Dead-Eye's section melted into the darkness, Finn said, 'Get some kip. I'll keep watch. Saraband'll be on the move well before dawn, and we'll follow him to Abbot's Cove, or rather, to the ruined monastery atop the headland. It overlooks the harbour. Who knows, Brains, there may be a chance to use your rockets after all!'

13 Disaster

'There they are!'

A mouse from the Dirty Squad was pointing excitedly. Far out to sea, just visible in the pale dawn light, two ships were approaching. A moment later, a roar burst from the rats below in the village as they, too, spotted their ships.

From his hiding place among the ruins up on the headland, Finn was casting anxious glances along the coast. Although the city was hidden by a low hill, the Great Fortress of Aramon was clearly outlined against the rising sun; but there was no sign of the Cardinal's ships.

'Don't worry, Boss,' said Brains. 'The tide's goin' out, and there's a stiff off-shore wind. Them ships'll take most of the day to reach the 'arbour.'

The hours crawled by. Finn ordered Brains to prepare his rockets. The rest of the Squad lay concealed among the ruins, their rifles trained on the rats below. The sun climbed to its zenith, but still no sign of the war galleons from Aramon. By mid-afternoon, the enemy ships were still a good way out, tacking against wind and tide to reach the harbour. They were drawing nearer and nearer.

'Boss! Look!'

With all sails spread and bright banners streaming, the three great warships seemed to fill the ocean! As they swept past the headland, their gun-ports flew open, and long cannon were rolled out, ready for action!

'They're alterin' course!' cried Brains. 'They're sailin' out to attack!'

In the village, the rats watched in a tense silence. Their own ships seemed paralyzed as the three warships sped triumphantly towards them. A shot crashed out from the leading warship, but the enemy was still out of range. 'Any minute now,' murmured Brains, his eyes gleaming. 'Why don't the rats' ships move?'

'They don't need to,' said Finn quietly. 'Oh, Lord o' Light! Will you look at that!'

The three warships were slowing, the wind spilling from their sails. At the same moment, the rats' ships sprang to life and surged forward. One of them swung round until it was broadside on to the nearest warship. Then it vanished in billows of smoke, as all its starboard guns roared at once.

The stricken warship reeled, and tried to claw its way out to the open sea, but in those few seconds, the wind had changed, the tide had turned, and the rats' ships were steadily herding their enemies away from the harbour, towards the rocks at the foot of the headland.

Another broadside roared across the sea, and the second warship seemed to shiver. Slowly, its mainmast toppled, dragging sails and rigging over the side. The third warship was out of control, its sails flapping uselessly. The rats' ships did not fire again: they had no need. Wind and tide were carrying the three warships to destruction.

Finn snapped into action. 'Silence! Get your section down the cliffs. When the ships strike the rocks, throw your ropes and try and save as many sea-mice as you can! Brains! Stand by to fire your rockets at the village! Burglar! Your section and Brains's mice, get down the slope! Keep those rats' heads down! They've seen what's happened. We've got to get those sea-mice away!'

The enemy ships were swinging away from the rocks; Finn could see small figures scurrying up the rigging and out along the spars to take in sail as the anchors thundered down. Gunsmoke billowed across the headland as the Dirty Squad opened fire, but the noise was drowned by a rending crash as the three warships struck the rocks.

Silence's mice were hurling lines to the helpless sea-mice. Through the flying spray, Finn saw several struggling ashore. But even as they began to scale the slope to safety, Finn realized that the rats were coming.

'Burglar!' he yelled. 'Keep firing, but fall back on the ruins if those devils get too close! Then take the cliff path to Aramon, and hold 'em off as long as you can!'

The first sea-mice were struggling up to the headland. 'Back to the city!' cried Finn. 'We'll cover you! Brains, get them rockets up!'

A young sea-mouse appeared, his gorgeous officer's uniform saturated and dripping. 'Thank you!' he gasped. 'Who are you?'

'Finn M'Conal, Captain of the Dirty Squad. Where's your commander? Doesn't he know anything about the tides and winds around here? The Cardinal will have his guts!'

'He's dead,' replied the mouse bleakly.

'Oh. Sorry . . . Look, get your lads to Aramon, fast! The rats'll be here any second!'

The young mouse staggered away, his face contorted with misery. Finn turned to Brains. 'Are those rockets ready? Then let 'em go!'

Brains struck flint and steel and ignited the long fuse. A sizzling – a whoosh – and a dozen rockets powered into the sky. Six fell among the rats packed in the village square, exploding with an ear-splitting crash. Rats scattered in all directions, and the terrified Red Kites rose into the air, squawking frantically, refusing to take any further part in the battle. Five more rockets plunged harmlessly into the sea, but the sixth struck the nearest enemy ship, and its sails and rigging vanished in a thunderous roar.

The rats faltered, but Saraband was urging them on. The Dirty Squad fell back in good order, firing steadily on the enemy. By now, all the sea-mice who could be saved were sprinting along the path towards the city. The Dirty Squad was using the cover of the ruins to hold back the rats, giving the sailors as much time as possible to escape.

'Back!' yelled Finn. He had seen more rats rapidly climbing the slope on his flank; they were trying to surround him. His mice left the ruins and dashed to the mouth of the narrow path that dipped behind the cliff's edge, forming a natural tunnel protected on the landward side by thick gorse and coils of bramble. As Finn was checking that all his mice were clear of the headland, he heard a whoosh and a roar, as another flight of rockets swept across the ruins towards the advancing rats.

'Brains! Leave it now! Come back!'

Brains grinned round at him. 'One more flight, Boss. Don't bother waitin'.'

'Brains! Come back *now*! That's an order!'

'Sure, Boss, just when I've —'

Another flight of rockets streaked towards the rats, who fled in terror. But from the right, Gobtooth's warriors suddenly surged across the headland. Brains swung round, levelled his rifle and fired. But as Finn watched in agony, Brains was overwhelmed by sheer weight of numbers.

Finn ran along the path. Bullets were flying

overhead and again and again he halted his mice to fire on the enemy. At last, the path ended. Across the open plain, lay Aramon.

The Dirty Squad halted, ready to fire as the rats burst from the path. But at that moment, as the first sea-mice were pelting across the plain, the big guns on the roof of the Great Fortress opened fire.

Massive round-shot shrieked overhead and ploughed into the brambles along the path, showering the rats with earth and stones. 'Come on!' screamed Saraband, for the city gates were open. Only the Dirty Squad stood between him and Aramon.

As the big guns roared again, a bugle sounded from the city and a horde of armed citizens poured out on to the plain. Swiftly, they formed ranks and fanned out, facing the oncoming rats. The Dirty Squad pelted up to them, flung themselves flat and were just in time to join in a devastating volley that drove the rats back in headlong flight, and not even Saraband could get them to advance again.

The Dirty Squad trudged wearily along the streets. Mice leant from their windows, cheering and waving. But Finn and his soldiers could not raise even a smile in return. As they reached the broad open space that lay in front of the Great Fortress, Dead-Eye and his section ran to greet them.

'Boss! Praise to the Lord o' Light you're safe! But what a foul-up! The Cardinal's furious . . . Boss? Where's Brains?'

The look in his comrades' eyes was answer enough. Dead-Eye turned away, swept up in the misery that had engulfed them all.

Brains was dead. And Saraband, when his undamaged ship had towed the other crippled vessel into harbour, had all the siege-guns he needed.

14 Aramon Besieged

That night, the mice watching anxiously from the city walls saw lights moving in the darkness. By daybreak, Saraband's siege-guns were in position, and his army was encamped in a wide semicircle, cutting off the city. Beyond the harbour, the rats' undamaged ship kept up a ceaseless patrol.

Once they had established their siege-line, the rats began scouring the nearby farms for food, driving yet more country-mice to take shelter in the city. Saraband let them through, reckoning that the more mouths there were to feed, the quicker starvation would force the mice into surrender.

His big siege-guns were half buried in trenches, out of range of the city's guns, and protected by tall, wickerwork shields and by the spells cast by the priests of the Sable Lord. Each night, the rats extended those trenches towards the city. Each morning, the guns had crept a little closer.

On the third morning, Cardinal Odo ordered that the cannon on the roof of the Great Fortress open fire. But the siege-guns were difficult to hit and most of the shots fell short, or screeched harmlessly over the rats' heads. Suddenly, three of Saraband's guns flamed and roared. The Great Fortress took a battering as the rats struggled to perfect their aim. By midday, the guns on the Fortress roof were shattered.

For the next three days, the rain sluiced down. It grew colder and colder, yet the rats toiled on through the waterlogged trenches, inching ever closer to the walls. On the third night, a hard frost turned the ground to iron and by morning it was snowing. Finn watched from the battlements, and he saw what Saraband was going to do.

The strong Gatehouse in the north wall would be difficult to batter down but, further along, the old ramparts took a sudden dip; the foundations were weak, and patches of mould had spread between the stones. It was an obvious spot for Saraband to attack. Through the swirling snow, Finn saw two great gouts of flame; a second later, came the cannons' roar. The mice flinched as iron round-shot crashed against the wall.

All morning, the defenders crouched against the battlements, watching helplessly. Labouring in relays, the rats loaded and fired until their guns were so hot that the falling snow sizzled and steamed on their barrels. 'Aim low!' ordered Saraband. Shot after shot thudded against the base of the wall until at last, with a loud groan, it collapsed. When the choking dust had settled, the mice saw a mountain of rubble. It rose almost to the height of the battlements on either side, but its gentle slope would provide the rats with a pathway into the city.

The siege-guns had fallen silent. In the narrow street behind the rubble, Finn and his mice were ready for the attack they knew would come. Up on the ramparts, to either side of the breach, the garrison silently stood to arms. Cardinal Odo fixed his eyes on the distant rats. Suddenly, he raised his club. It was the signal.

'*Come on, lads*!' cried Finn. The Dirty Squad

dashed forward and clambered up the rubble, already slippery with snow. Finn had taken over Brains's section; he halted them at the top, while Dead-Eye, Silence and Burglar led their mice slithering down the slope, seeking cover amid the tumbled stones. Across the snowy plain, a body of rats was charging towards them.

'*The wall's down*!' yelled Saraband. He turned to Karabas, whose eyes were sparkling with excitement. 'Now, Lord King! Lead your warriors into the city!'

'What?' squeaked Karabas, a wave of terror washing over him. All week, he had been urging Saraband to launch an attack, but he never dreamt that he would be expected to lead it.

The warriors were watching him expectantly. 'Come, my lord!' cried Saraband. 'Here's your chance. Our Kings always lead their warriors into battle. Surely you will not *refuse*?'

Karabas was trapped. Already, the warriors were nudging one another and sneering. 'Of course I'll do it!' he exclaimed indignantly, wishing the ground would open up and swallow him. 'Er – how many warriors can I take?'

Saraband smiled. 'Oh, with you to lead them,

you won't need many . . . Two hundred?'

Karabas felt sick. He had hoped for half the army at least. But when Saraband agreed to send in a flight of Red Kites as well, he had to give in. Drawing his sword, and trying to look brave, he ordered his warriors to advance.

As he drew near to the breach, his confidence returned. The ramparts were silent. The breach appeared to be undefended. As the Red Kites swooped overhead, Karabas waved his sword. 'Onwards, my brave rats! Onwards to victory!'

Suddenly, the walls erupted in smoke and flame. From the breach, Dead-Eye's section fired, then Burglar's. Silence's mice were blazing away at the Red Kites, many of which fell to the ground, their riders dragged off as prisoners. The remainder wheeled and flew off in terror. By the time Finn's section had poured in their deadly volley, Dead-Eye's mice had reloaded and the rats reeled as the disciplined fire shredded their ranks.

'Oh, help!' cried Karabas. 'Back! Retreat!' But the warriors could not hear him above the crash of gunfire and had no intention of retreating anyway. Karabas found himself swept to the very foot of the pile of rubble, the Dirty Squad's bullets zinging round him.

As the undaunted warriors began to climb the slope, Dead-Eye's section dropped their rifles, drew their daggers and hurled themselves at the rats, stabbing, scratching, biting, tearing, yelling and screaming. The rats faltered. And the snow turned red.

'Tell the Cardinal we need fifty mice from the walls!' yelled Finn. But Odo was already directing eager mice to help the Dirty Squad. As the reinforcements arrived, Finn ordered them down the slope, where Burglar's mice were fighting ferociously alongside Dead-Eye's. Silence was directing his section to fire over their heads into the densely packed warriors still waiting to attack.

'Look out!' screamed a mouse as a second flight of Red Kites swooped through the falling snow. Silence felt a sudden searing pain in his sword-arm as a savage beak tore into it. Finn took swift aim, fired, and the huge bird fell dead. But Silence was down, and his mice were forming a circle round him, hacking, stabbing at the enemy, and ripping with teeth and claws. Now the rats were attacking in overwhelming numbers. Gradually, fighting every inch of the way, the Dirty Squad was forced back up the slope. Karabas and his warriors scented victory.

'Back!' yelled Finn. 'All of you! Back into the city!'

Slipping and slithering, the mice turned tail and fled up the slope. Tumbling, falling down the far side, they dashed for the shelter of the streets. Turning once more to face the breach, they swiftly reloaded and waited tensely for the rats to appear.

'Come on!' yelled Karabas. 'We've won!' The cheering rats followed him until the outer slope was thick with advancing warriors. But, as they reached the crest, they heard a loud whooshing sound; from far down the street, trails of fire were streaking towards them!

CRASH! The rockets struck the top of the slope, exploding with a deafening roar. Stones flew upwards, the rats yelled in terror and, from the streets below, the Dirty Squad poured in a deadly volley.

A second flight of rockets soared above the rats' heads, exploding with a rending crash against the outer slope.

'Back!' yelled Karabas. 'BACK!'

The rats pelted back down the slope. 'Come on, lads!' screamed Finn, and the Dirty Squad once more hurled themselves up the pile of rubble. Reaching the top, they saw the rats fleeing in disarray. The mice gave them one more volley for luck, then they hastened to help their wounded comrades. From all along the ramparts, mice were cheering, laughing, and crying with relief. They had won.

But only because Brains's section still had their dead leader's rockets, which Finn had prepared in case the rats should overwhelm the breach. Now he had used them all up, and could make no more, since Brains had never written down his invention. As Finn peered through the falling snow towards the huge army that still encircled them, he wondered how much longer the city could hold out. Burglar touched his arm. 'Boss. Silence's hurt. You'd better come . . .'

Their heads bowed in shame, the warriors stood before Saraband's tent, silently enduring his bitter tongue-lashing. 'You miserable, cowardly vermin! Afraid of a few bangs? You're not fit to be called warriors. You had a victory and you threw it away. Get out of my sight!' Bitterly ashamed, the rats turned away. 'Wait. Where's Karabas?'

A group of warriors slunk up to him. They were carrying something. As they laid it down and crept away, Saraband found himself looking down at the dead body of their King. He turned aside, so that the warriors should not see his smile. Entering his tent, he rubbed his paws with glee. Of course, he had known that the breach would be strongly defended; he had not expected a victory. That was why he had sent Karabas, so that he should suffer the shame of defeat. But, by a stupendous stroke of luck, Karabas was dead. Now, Saraband had only to wait for the moment of victory for his warriors to hail him as their King.

Part Three

The Sword and the Crown

15 Wiglaff

Rufus was running for his life. Tall trees with out-stretched skeletal, limbs tried to bar his way, dangling twigs raked his face and tendrils of mist snaked about his feet, hiding the spiteful coils of bramble that tried to trip him. Somewhere ahead, Elana was fleeing with the precious Chalice, but the moles were gaining on them, their pounding feet echoing the thudding of Rufus's heart. He was gasping; the freezing air burnt his lungs. He staggered on leaden feet, and as he tripped and sprawled, the moles surrounded him, a brutal kick thudded into his side and a voice yelled, 'Wake up, slave!'

Rufus groaned. The dream was fading, but the pain in his side told him that the kick had been real enough. The moles hauled him up, and dragged him from his cell to the end of a short tunnel.

'Start digging, slave. There's worms a-plenty in there, and we'll expect your bowl to be full when we get back, or no breakfast.' The moles clumped off down the tunnel, but Rufus knew they would not go far. Sullenly, he began to dig. He was fed up with being insulted and ordered about by these blank-faced moles, but he sensed that they were waiting for an excuse to attack him, and he would stand no chance against so many. So, with an effort, he kept his temper.

In the Rats' Castle, he had at least been able to see daylight. Here, in his new slavery, he toiled, ate and slept in perpetual night. He had lost all sense of time. Worst of all, Elana was a prisoner somewhere else in this dark labyrinth. Though Rufus had no idea where she was, he was determined to rescue her.

His food was gathered from the woods by a little mole called Wiglaff. He was so clumsy that the cry of 'Oh, *Wiglaff*!' echoed frequently through the tunnels, as he dropped something or tripped over something. But Rufus noticed that Wiglaff rarely dropped his meagre ration of berries and nuts. He looked forward to the mole's visits, for Wiglaff hated Rhiannon and Oslaf, and whenever the guards were out of earshot, he would tell Rufus, in a breathless whisper, just what had been going on in the city. 'Rhiannon's always been jealous of Morganna. She and Oslaf must've been plotting together for ages.'

'Didn't Morganna suspect anything?'

'No. Well, nothing as bad as this. None of us did. But now we know that Oslaf's been bribing warriors to take his side against Rothgar, and make Rhiannon Queen. As for poor Morganna, goodness knows where she is, but rumour has it Rhiannon's starving her to death. Of course, your arrival was a stroke of luck for Rhiannon.'

'How?'

'Well, she took advantage of Rothgar's absence on the Treasure hunt to imprison her sister, helped by some of the rebel warriors. Oslaf, meanwhile, followed Rothgar and killed him. And, of course, Rhiannon had to take you two prisoner.'

'Why?'

'Because she wanted the Chalice, and you're its guardian. I don't know why she wants it, but I'm very much afraid she'll put it to some evil use . . .'

*

In the dead of night, Rufus awoke and flung out a paw to defend himself against the shadow looming over him, and a voice whispered, 'It's me!'

'Wiglaff! I thought you were one of the warriors. What's the matter? What are you doing here?'

The little mole was bubbling with excitement. 'Listen! I've found out that Morganna's in a dungeon, deep below the city – and Elana's with her. I think I can get them out. At least, I'm going to try.'

Rufus hesitated. Was this a trap?

Wiglaff saw the doubt in the mouse's eyes. 'Please trust me,' he begged, looking so desolate that Rufus grinned. What had he to lose?

'I trust you. But how are you going to get them out?'

'The dungeons are well guarded, but there's a passage that runs close behind Morganna's cell. If I can get down there without being seen, I can tunnel into her cell and get them both away from the city.'

'But all exits are guarded.'

'Ah, but at the centre of the city is the fortress. All mole cities have one. It's a big cavern where warriors assemble in times of danger. It's a holy place, too. We meet there once a month to pray to the Lord of Light. It's close to the surface; you can see tree roots in the roof. I can easily tunnel out. But I'm a bit scared to do it all on my own. Could you – ?'

'Yes. Just tell me what to do!'

'Well, tomorrow Rhiannon and Oslaf are giving a banquet in the Council Chamber. All moles are summoned, except for a few who have to stay on guard duty. Rhiannon's going to announce something important. I'm afraid it has to do with the Chalice, and it's going to be very bad indeed. We must get away before it happens. When you come off your second shift of worm-gathering, I'll meet you here. Once we've got Morganna and Elana out, we'll use the Inner Ring-tunnel to reach the fortress.'

'But that means leaving the Chalice.'

'Rufus, don't worry about the Chalice. If we can get away, there are moles in other cities who will help us get it back.'

'All right. But tell me how to reach the fortress in case we are separated.'

'You remember the Council Chamber? Well, past that, there's a tunnel to the right that slopes upwards; it leads to the Inner Ring-tunnel, so follow it to the end, then remember to turn left. Take the next passage but one to the right, and that takes you to the fortress.'

Rufus made Wiglaff repeat the directions three times, and hoped he would not have to follow them alone.

Next day the hours crawled by. During his second shift, Rufus became aware of unusual activity in the city. His bowls of worms were taken away more frequently than usual, and the guards kept ordering him to work faster.

At last, weary and covered in earth, he was told to stop, and a guard led him back to his cell. There, he waited tensely. At last, a mole appeared in the entrance. But it was not Wiglaff.

'You. Slave. Come with me.'

'Where?' snarled Rufus.

'Council Chamber,' replied the blank-faced warrior. 'Big banquet. You're wanted to serve wine and worms. Queen's orders.'

Rufus was tempted to fly at the mole, knock him down and run for it. But he knew there would be other guards nearby so, with a sinking heart, he walked slowly out of his cell. As he was escorted down the tunnel, he saw Wiglaff hastening towards him. It was too dark to see the mole's face, but Rufus could imagine its stricken expression. As he entered the Council Chamber, he wondered whether Wiglaff would have the nerve to carry out the rescue alone.

'Oh, Lord of Light,' he prayed. 'Give him the courage to do it! At least Elana will be out of this dreadful place!'

16 Peril Under Ground

Rufus was kept frantically busy, carrying bowls of worms and jugs of wine to the feasting moles. At least he could see what he was doing, for the Chamber was lit by smoky, foul-smelling lamps. Rufus noticed that several moles were eating and drinking in silence. Perhaps they were still secretly loyal to Morganna.

Rhiannon and Oslaf sat together on a raised platform at the far end of the Chamber. The new Queen was dripping with jewels. In front of her stood the Chalice. Oslaf slouched in his seat, one paw clamped round the hilt of his dagger, his watchful eyes roving up and down the Chamber. At last, Rhiannon rose to her feet. Instantly, there was silence.

'The bad old days are over. I promise you a time of peace and plenty. All moles will live in harmony. All I ask is obedience to me and to my dear Lord Oslaf.'

Most of the warriors cheered. But Rufus noticed some moles clenching their paws and glaring down at the table. The Queen raised her paw for silence.

'In my sister's time, we worshipped the Lord of Light. But no longer! He is a weak and feeble god, fit only to be worshipped by mice! From now on, we shall worship a strong god. The god of the rats. The Sable Lord of Darkness!'

Oh, you fool, thought Rufus. You don't know what you're doing!

Rhiannon went on, 'When we have seen the Sable Lord himself, and received his blessing, we shall leave these stinking tunnels and join the rats. Think of it, my warriors. A little fighting, a little blooding of our swords and axes, and all the riches of Aramon shall be ours!'

The excited moles hammered their daggers on the tables. But they fell silent as Rhiannon took up the Chalice. Rufus now realized with horror just why she had wanted it. She would use it to summon the Sable Lord.

Rhiannon's eyes glittered as she raised the Chalice.

'By earth and iron,
Fire and water,
Claw and tooth,
Axe and sword –
We the Mole-Kind call upon you:
Reveal yourself, O, Sable Lord!'

An icy wind swept round the Chamber. Every light, save one, went out. Rufus crept closer to the high table. He knew what was going to happen and waited, fearful and angry. What terrible madness had taken hold of Rhiannon? He had to take the Chalice now. He couldn't risk leaving it for someone else to rescue.

As the moles trembled in the darkness, a swirl of mist appeared above them. Inside it, something was moving; something that grew and took shape until suddenly it was revealed in all its horror.

It was a huge mole, with blazing eyes, claws like daggers, and jaws that dripped with blood.

Remembering the giant rat he had seen in Zagora's castle, Rufus guessed that the Sable Lord had sent another Dark Angel, this time in the shape of the creature who had summoned him. Rufus wondered what the Sable Lord really looked like, but he pushed away the thought, for the dark god's power was flooding the chamber; Rufus fixed his eyes on the Chalice and filled his mind with light.

At the appearance of the great mole, the warriors had cried in terror and hidden their faces. But Rhiannon was gazing at the creature with shining eyes. 'Give us strength to overcome the mice of Carminel!' she cried. 'Give us the Treasures of Aramon and take this treasure in exchange!'

She raised the Chalice. The Dark Angel's eyes gleamed in triumph as it reached out its claws.

Rufus tore the Chalice from Rhiannon and sprinted down the Chamber. With a furious roar, the Dark Angel swept after him. Rufus felt it looming above him as he fled between the long tables towards the doorway. The guards were reaching out to stop him. The creature's foul, hot breath blasted his face, its cruel eyes burnt into his skull. Rufus hurled the Chalice with all his strength, straight at the Dark Angel's head.

A blinding light, a deafening roar and the

creature vanished with a hideous smell of burning. Rhiannon was screeching with fury; Oslaf was lumbering down the Chamber. The Chalice had struck the roof and was falling straight into Rufus's outstretched paws.

'Stop him!' screamed Rhiannon, but the guards at the door were still blinded by the searing light. Rufus dodged past them and dashed down the passage. Rhiannon's screams rang in his ears, and the ground beneath his feet was thudding as Oslaf and his moles pounded in pursuit.

As Rufus fled, he wondered whether Wiglaff had carried out the rescue alone. He hoped so. His only chance was to make for the fortress. Maybe he would be able to tunnel out. His paws were certainly stronger now, after all that digging for worms!

He almost missed the turning. Skidding to a halt, he darted beneath the low arch, and pelted up the slope, desperately trying to remember Wiglaff's directions. He paused for breath. Though the shouting had faded, the earth still trembled to the pounding of feet. The vibrations seemed to surround him, and for a moment he pictured the labyrinth of the moles' city, in which he might wander for ever . . .

He pulled himself together. He felt again the tingling sensation as the power of the Chalice flowed into him. He grinned as he remembered how it had destroyed the Dark Angel and he wondered what it would do to the rats. Resolving to die rather than let it go again, Rufus plunged onwards into the darkness.

At last, the tunnel ended, and he sensed another, much broader passage, stretching across his path. The Inner Ring-tunnel! But . . . which way must he go? Once again, the earth gave warning: the moles were closing in. Blindly he swung to the right, crashing into walls as the tunnel curved inwards, seeking the turning that would lead him to the fortress. The shouts seemed to be coming from in front as well as behind. He stopped, and tried to calm his gasping breath. His legs were trembling with exhaustion. He closed his eyes, willing himself to go on. When he opened them, he saw that the rim of the Chalice was faintly glowing, and there, to his left, was another passage.

Rufus had lost all sense of direction. He dashed headlong into the new tunnel. As he ran, so the light from the Chalice gradually intensified, until he could see the tunnel walls, and the worms that crawled in and out of them. Suddenly the tunnel divided. Again, he sensed vibrations through the earth.

Choosing a tunnel at random, Rufus dashed down it. But the light from the Chalice was fading, and he heard distant shouts ahead. He turned and fled back. He took the other tunnel and, as he stumbled and staggered, gasping for breath, the light from the Chalice grew brighter. At last, he was aware of an airy lightness above and around him. Small rushlights defined a cavern. Huddled together in the centre were Morganna and Elana.

Rufus had missed Elana so badly that for a moment he could not believe that he had found her. She rushed into his arms, crying with relief. But even as he hugged her, and felt his own tears surging up, he knew he must not relax. Over by the wall there was a sudden scrabbling and a mole was running towards him. Rufus pushed Elana aside as he confronted this new danger.

'*Wiglaff*!'

'You made it!' cried the little mole.

'Just about,' said Rufus. 'But they're after me.'

Wiglaff frowned and shook his head. 'The Queen's so weak she can't dig. I've made a start, but the roof's thicker than I thought.' He scampered back to his tunnel. Rufus looked at Elana. She was thin, and her clothes, like his, were ragged and filthy. But her eyes were shining. Suddenly, Rufus heard the sound he had been dreading – shouts and running feet. Taking Elana's paw, he stood protectively over the huddled figure of the Queen. Morganna was lying against a sort of stone altar. She looked up at Rufus. 'My dear,' she murmured faintly, 'have you any water?'

Rufus knelt beside her. 'No. I'm sorry.' He glanced down at the glowing Chalice. It was full of wine. Greatly wondering, he held it to the Queen's lips. Morganna drank. When she raised her head, a light had been rekindled in her eyes. 'Thank you, Rufus. How good to see you again! I feel much better for that. But where is Wiglaff?'

'Tunnelling out. He'll be ready soon. *Elana – listen*!'

The shouts were drawing nearer. Rufus yelled to Wiglaff to hurry. But there was no reply.

'Oslaf is coming,' said Morganna calmly. 'I think we need some protection.'

'Yes, but what?' Rufus was staring at the entrance to the cavern. Any second now . . .

'Well, you have the Chalice,' said Morganna. 'Now you need the Sword.'

Suddenly, Rufus understood. 'Elana! The poem!

Remember? *Under a fortress the Sword is concealed*. This is the fortress!'

Morganna was sharpening her claws against the stone altar. 'The secret of the Sword is known only to the reigning monarch of this city. Lord Gideon was a friend of the Mould-Warp; one of his castles, an old tower, stands close by. When Gideon sensed his death was near, he entrusted his Sword to us. He believed that if Carminel were ever in danger, the Sword would be safer underground, where it would be found, at last, by the right mouse at the right time. Only the Lord of Light would have granted you the Chalice; I think he wants you to have the Sword also – and I hope you know how to use it.'

So do I, thought Rufus. Morganna began to dig. But now the mice realized that there were many entrances to the fortress and each one was dimly outlined with torchlight as the moles closed in.

'A little more of that wine, please,' said Morganna. 'Ah, that's much better. Now we shan't be long!' The Chalice was gleaming brightly. The old mole scrabbled in the earth. Suddenly, she was still. 'It's gone!'

From all round the cavern, the moles burst in. Oslaf strode over to Morganna and yanked her to her feet. Two warriors flung themselves on the mice. Rufus and Elana scratched and bit, struggled and kicked, but they could not break the grip of those mighty paws. Flanked by torch-bearing moles, Rhiannon swept into the fortress. At the sight of the Queen, she let out a peal of laughter.

'Digging for Treasure, sister dear? Is this what you were looking for?'

Morganna and the mice stared in dismay. Rhiannon was holding a magnificent, jewelled sword.

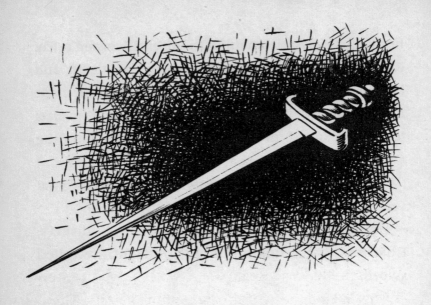

17 The Sword of Gideon

Bound and gagged, Rufus was hauled into the
Council Chamber. In the dim rushlight, he could
see Elana and Morganna in the same helpless state.
Rhiannon sat enthroned, the great Sword at her
waist, the Chalice at her feet. She was guarded by
her warriors, and Oslaf towered at her side. Just in
front of her stood a low chopping block.

'Oslaf and I have been discussing your fate,' she
announced with a smile. 'The Sable Lord is angry,
and must be appeased: only then will he give his
blessing on our march to Aramon. So, our sister shall

return to prison, where she will suffer death by starvation. Oh, sister dear, did you really think that I didn't know about the Sword? You must be even more foolish than you look. The Sword will help us to victory! As for you, mice, you've been nothing but trouble since you arrived. You will die.' She turned to one of her warriors. 'Is your axe sharp? Good, get on with it, then. Behead them both at the same time. That will be interesting.'

Her peal of laughter echoed round the Chamber. But the mole was looking uncertain. 'I don't reckon as how we ought to, if it please your majesty. These mice are under the protection of the Lord of Light. Oh, I know we don't worship him no more,' he added hastily, seeing Rhiannon's expression, 'but he's still mighty powerful, and –'

'Treason!' screamed Rhiannon. 'Blasphemy! Tie him up. He can die with the mice.'

Two warriors seized the mole, bound his paws and flung him down beside Rufus and Elana. He was whimpering with terror. 'No, your majesty, please, no!'

'Shut up! Oslaf, kill them all. The mice first, then that miserable mole.'

Oslaf smiled and hefted his axe. At his signal, two warriors pushed the mice towards the chopping block. 'Remove their gags,' commanded Rhiannon. 'It'll be amusing to hear them beg for mercy.'

As the filthy rag was torn from her mouth, Elana glared furiously at Rhiannon. 'One day these moles will come to their senses and drive you out for ever!' she snarled. 'And that murderer beside you!'

'Fat chance!' Rhiannon laughed, and looked at Rufus. 'Well, mouse?'

Rufus looked at the beautiful face and its hard, gleaming eyes. 'You can kill us if it amuses you. But you cannot put the Treasures to evil use. The Dark Angel could not bear the Chalice's touch and the Sword will turn against you rather than let itself be used against the Mouse-Kind. As for Saraband – he'll use you, then destroy you.'

'Enough!' Rhiannon was trembling with rage. 'Go on, Oslaf, *kill them*! *Kill them now*!'

Two warriors closed in and, untying the mice, forced them to their knees. They struggled to the last, even when they felt the rough wood of the chopping block against their necks. 'Other mice will come and take the Treasures!' yelled Rufus. 'You'll never be safe as long as you –'

'*Kill them*!' screamed Rhiannon. The glittering blade swung up. Rufus glared at Olslaf and wondered why he suddenly looked so surprised. He flung himself and Elana out of the way of the falling axe as Oslaf collapsed with a terrible cry. The mice saw a mole standing in one of the entrances, holding a smoking pistol.

'*Wiglaff*!'

Suddenly, the Chamber was swarming with armed warriors. In their midst, his head bandaged, stood Rothgar.

Rhiannon screamed. 'I thought you were dead. Oslaf said —'

'It would take more than Oslaf to kill me,' growled Rothgar, 'although he wounded me badly and left me for dead. But Wiglaff found me in the forest, while he was gathering food for Rufus. He bound up my wounds and tended me day and night.'

'Traitor!' screamed Rhiannon. Rothgar ignored her.

'I swore Wiglaff to secrecy. But he knew which moles were loyal, and one by one they've been slipping away to join me. Didn't you notice?'

'I couldn't tell you about Rothgar,' said Wiglaff to the mice. 'But last night, when you were captured, Oslaf's moles didn't know I was there, so I burrowed out and went to Rothgar and the others. He gave me this pistol. Never thought I'd have to use it.'

'Disarm these traitors and release Queen Morganna,' ordered Rothgar. The rebel warriors were hopelessly outnumbered. Surrendering their swords and axes, they stood with bowed heads. 'Why is that warrior tied up?'

'He refused to execute us,' said Rufus. 'It took courage to stand up to Rhiannon. We're grateful to him.'

'And so am I. Untie him.' Rothgar turned to Rhiannon. 'Unbuckle that Sword! It belongs to Rufus.'

Rhiannon obeyed, but as the belt slid from her waist, she drew the Sword and, with a cry of 'Murderer!', she leapt at Wiglaff, who flinched and flung up his paws as the long blade came glittering down. A clash of steel, a blaze of light – and Rhiannon's scream of agony was drowned in a roar of thunder. When Rufus opened his eyes, he saw that Wiglaff was unharmed, but Rhiannon was lying still.

Rothgar knelt beside her. 'She will live,' he said. 'It is up to Queen Morganna to decide her fate, and the fate of those warriors who followed her. Oslaf is dead, justly slain by Wiglaff to save his friends.'

Trembling, the rebels knelt to Morganna and bowed their heads in submission. The Queen regarded them sternly. 'You are all guilty of high treason. I will spare your lives, but you are banished from this city. Leave your weapons, and go to the farthest corner of the wood. There you may dig your own city, and I shall tell the other moles who dwell beneath the forest what kind of creatures you are.'

As the loyal moles escorted the crestfallen rebels away, Rufus asked Morganna, 'What will you do with Rhiannon?'

Morganna sighed. 'She deserves to die. But she is my sister. I will keep her in prison until she comes to her senses . . . If she ever does.'

Rothgar picked up the Sword and gazed at it in wonder. 'I know not what power lies in this . . .'

But Rufus did. Just as Rhiannon had raised the Sword to strike at Wiglaff, Rufus had seen, for a moment, a mouse with a long, curved snout, and wearing a scarlet cloak. With his upraised sword, he had deflected the savage cut that would otherwise have cloven Wiglaff's skull. Then the mouse had vanished. But Rufus had guessed who he was: Gideon, Eagle Warrior, whose spirit still kept watch over his mice, and who would not allow his Sword to be used for evil.

'Take the Sword, Rufus,' said Rothgar, 'and the Chalice. There is news in the forest that Saraband is laying siege to Aramon – you and your Treasures will be needed if the Rat-Kind are not to enslave us all.'

Elana flung her paws round Wiglaff and hugged him. Rufus grasped his paw. 'How can we ever thank you? You've saved our lives. I only hope that I can do the same for you some day.'

'Wiglaff's courage deserves the highest reward,' said Queen Morganna. 'From now on, he will be my Chief Adviser. Rufus and Elana: if ever you are in danger, send for the moles. Our tunnels run to the edges of the forest, and any woodland creature will guide you to us. Now you must go, and may the Lord of Light protect you, for the fate of Carminel depends on you.'

18 The Raid

From a narrow window, high in the Great Fortress, Captain Finn was looking out over the rooftops of Aramon towards the ring of campfires twinkling in the darkness. An icy wind was blowing, bearing rich cooking smells that set Finn's empty belly grumbling with hunger. In the overcrowded city, food supplies were running low. Aramon was close to starvation.

Cardinal Odo entered the room and sat heavily at his desk. He looked tired and thinner. But his eyes still smiled. 'Put another log on the fire, Finn, before we freeze to death.' It was the last one.

Firewood was as strictly rationed as food, and the Cardinal's private room was no exception. 'You know what day it is today, Finn? The Birthday of the Lord of Light. A time for feasting.' Odo smiled sadly. 'But there'll be no feasting tonight.'

'No, sir. But at least we'll still have the lights at midnight.'

All over Carminel, on the stroke of twelve, the mice would run eagerly outside to watch the explosion of natural fireworks in the sky. Streaks of multicoloured light, soaring into the heavens and pouring towards the earth: a fabulous display of energy and power, a never-failing promise that the Lord of Light still lived, and was watching over them.

'Ah, yes, the lights at midnight,' rumbled the Cardinal. 'And before that, our mice will be gathering to celebrate the Birthday. I shall be in the Great Cathedral with all those who are not guarding the walls. But, tonight, there will be no singing. Instead, we shall hold a solemn vigil and pray to the god to deliver us from the curse of Saraband.'

'Good idea, sir.'

'But you won't be there, Finn. I've got a job for you. Those siege-guns that made the breach: I want you to destroy them before they make another

120

breach in the wall. How you do it is up to you, but do it! The lights in the sky should distract the rats. They've seen them before, of course, but they should remind those vermin that their Sable Lord isn't all-powerful.'

'Very good, sir.' Finn sounded more confident than he felt.

'Take two sections. We dare not risk any more. And try not to lose any of them. Your Squad did well today. How's Silence?'

'He'll live, sir. But his sword-arm's paralyzed. He'll not fight again.'

'If I know Silence, he'll fight with his other arm. But I'm sorry he's hurt. I'll go and see him later. Go now, and the best of luck.'

As Finn left the Great Fortress, an idea struck him. He hastened through the city to an old dock-side tavern, The Cardinal's Head. There he found Burglar, Dead-Eye and their sections eating a meagre supper of cold potatoes and mouldy cheese, washed down with stale beer. 'Buck up and finish that,' said Finn. 'We've a little job to do tonight.'

Finn, with Dead-Eye's section, was creeping across the snow. Burglar's mice were invisible, but Finn knew they were somewhere to his right. The night was dry, but dense clouds hid the stars. The only light came from the rats' campfires. The mice had left the city by boat, rowing up the Aramon River to a point well beyond the enemy's line. From there, they had trekked across country in a wide circle. Now, Finn and his comrades were crawling towards the campfire that marked the position of their target: the two big guns.

The absence of cover was no problem to the Dirty Squad. They silently burrowed into the snow, and waited for Burglar's section to go into action.

Snug in their blankets, Nym and Skillet were sitting by their campfire. Nearby, the two mighty siege-guns were silhouetted against the dark sky. 'Shame about Karabas,' said Nym.

'Yeah, poor old Karabas!' The two rats burst out laughing.

'Reckon Saraband'll be King now,' said Nym. 'And that'll mean rich pickings for the likes of us! Oh, Great Sable Lord! *What was that*?'

'Gunfire! From down the line; that's near Saraband's tent! Oh, blimey, them mice are attackin' us! Help! HELP!' Yelling frantically, the two rats stumbled through the snow. Another volley crashed out, bugles blared and, from both ends of the siege-line, rats were leaving their posts and pelting towards the firing.

'Well, that seems to have worked,' said Finn cheerfully. 'Where's Burglar?'

A mouse came panting out of the darkness and flung himself down beside his comrades, dropping his pack with a loud thud.

'Just what have you got in there?' asked Finn suspiciously.

'Oh, nuffink much!' Burglar's eyes were wide with innocence. His comrades grinned. Trust Burglar to turn a secret mission into a thieving expedition!

'All right, Burglar, you know what to do.'

From down the line came another crackle of gunfire, as Burglar's section kept up the pretence of an attack. But Finn knew that time was running out. Already the rats were blazing away at the trees where the mice lay concealed. He must not risk their lives. Burglar would have to hurry.

Keeping their heads down, Burglar and two mice from Dead-Eye's section sprinted across the snow towards the unguarded guns. Opening their packs, the mice took out what looked like long, thin sausages and passed them to Burglar, who started wrapping them round the barrel of the first gun. He worked swiftly, coiling the sausages round the wheels of the gun carriage before tying the loose ends together and leaving them lying on a patch of ground he had carefully cleared of snow. As he finished, two more mice dashed out, and Burglar wrapped more lengths of sausage round the barrel of the second gun. He tied the two trailing ends together, and reached for the powder flask held ready by one of his helpers.

The sausages were made of canvas, tightly packed with gunpowder. Burglar poured a measure of gunpowder over the joined ends. 'Fuse!'

A mouse passed him a coil of cord, smeared with pitch. Burglar tied it to the trailing ends of the sausages. 'GO!'

The mice ran. Burglar walked slowly back, uncoiling the cord, and brushing away the snow on either side of it. He was still some distance from his comrades when he realized that the firing from down the line had stopped. The rats were coming back. He crouched lower, still uncoiling the long cord, forcing himself to move slowly, as any rapid movement might be seen. Behind him, the mice held their breaths. It was almost midnight. The clouds had vanished, the stars were shining brightly. Any second now, the sky would erupt with light. But it might just be too late.

'You blithering idiot!' said Saraband, as he and Gobtooth, followed by Nym and Skillet, trudged towards the guns. 'How many times must I tell you? These mice are not fools. That attack on my tent was an obvious diversion; I wasn't even in it. So, what do you suppose the mice are up to?'

'Dunno,' replied Gobtooth sullenly.

'Oh, don't you? Well, how about using your brain for once? Sabotage, probably . . . Oh, Great Sable Lord! The guns! Gobtooth! Go back and check on all the guns down the line! You two imbeciles, come with me!'

As the rats broke into a stumbling run, Burglar slithered into his hole in the snow. Finn was striking flint and steel, but the wood shavings in his tinder-box were damp. Again and again he tried, but it was no use. The rats were almost up to the guns when Dead-Eye elbowed Finn aside, pointed his pistol at the end of the fuse, and fired.

Instantly, the rats flung themselves flat. They did not see the shadowy figures flitting away into the darkness, nor did they see the little flame, steadily advancing along the cord, creeping ever closer to the guns.

'Get up!' Saraband was wondering why there had been no more shots, when he spotted the low, creeping flame. 'Back!'

Nym and Skillet spun round, bumped into each

other and went sprawling. Saraband flung himself flat as the massive explosion tore the night apart. The guns leapt into the air. For a moment, their shattered pieces, outlined in a white-hot glare, hung suspended, then they crashed to the ground. As the dazed rats staggered to their feet, there came a second flash. The piles of powder barrels stacked nearby exploded in a roar that swept across the plain until it echoed from the city wall and rolled back to where the rats were cowering in terror.

With that explosion came another. The whole sky thundered, roared and exploded with light so dazzling that all along the line the rats hid their eyes, crying in terror to the Sable Lord. Comets, their glittering tails spreading in gold and silver showers, torrents of light cascading earthwards like glittering waterfalls and, above the city, a great star was blazing.

The Dirty Squad had gone into deep cover in a fir forest, well behind the siege-line. They stared in awe at the sky. The midnight lights had never been like this.

Burglar opened his pack. 'Here, lads. Fresh bread an' honey. Reckon we'll 'ave a feast after all.'

'Cor! Where d'you nick that from?' asked Dead-Eye.

Burglar winked and tapped his snout. 'Never you mind. Let's just say that old Saraband'll 'ave to find somethink else for 'is breakfast tomorrer!'

Laughing, the mice gathered round, their whiskers twitching. They had almost forgotten how hungry they were. The sweet smells filled their nostrils, and they settled down to watch the midnight lights, gorging themselves on the plundered food.

'Boss!' murmured Dead-Eye after a while. 'I think we've got company!'

'Cover!' snapped Finn. The Squad ducked out of sight behind the trees, rifles at the ready. 'But don't shoot!'

Two mice emerged from the shadows. Their clothes were mere rags, and their naked feet were cut and bleeding. One of the mice carried a bow and arrows, and was clutching a bundle to her breast. The other wore a long sword.

The Squad was invisible, but Rufus sensed its presence. He drew the Sword of Gideon, which sparkled in sudden brilliance. Finn glanced up. The lights were fading, but the great star, which had shone over Aramon, was blazing directly above them in the dark sky.

19 'Find the Eagles!'

Lighting a fire would be risky. But the night was bitterly cold, and Rufus and Elana were frozen. While Finn bathed the travellers' feet with melted snow from his pot, Dead-Eye and Burglar sorted out some warm clothing for them, dumped their filthy rags on the fire and gave them bread and honey.

'We've heard that Saraband is besieging Aramon,' said Rufus.

'So he is,' replied Finn. 'So far without success. His army lies just beyond this wood. But don't worry,' he added, seeing Elana's look of alarm, 'you're with the Special Operations Unit. We are the Dirty Squad, and you're safe with us.'

When Rufus and Elana were thoroughly warm and had licked the last of the honey from their paws, Rufus told their story. Finn and his comrades listened in growing astonishment. The fire faded to a heap of scarlet embers. But the little glade still basked in the light of the great star, whose silver rays sparked fire from the jewels in Rufus's Sword, and gleamed on his reddish-black fur.

'So you not only found two of the Treasures of Carminel,' said Finn, 'you also stopped that mad Rhiannon from joining up with Saraband. Lord o' Light! And I thought *we* led an adventurous life!'

'Do you two want to join the Dirty Squad?' asked Dead-Eye admiringly.

Rufus grinned, and shook his head. 'We still have one more Treasure to find.'

'The Crown,' said Elana. 'We're hoping Saraband has it with him. We might be able to get it if it's in his tent.'

'What's it like?' asked Burglar casually.

'Silver, with a big ruby in the centre,' said Rufus.

'Oh,' said Burglar. 'That's a pity.'

Finn eyed him suspiciously. 'And why is it a pity?'

Burglar looked embarrassed. 'Well, I saw it in Saraband's tent, while I was pinchin' the bread and honey. I thought it belonged to him. So I nicked it.'

'Lord o' Light!' exclaimed Finn. 'And what, may I ask, were you intendin' to do with it?'

'Flog it to the merchant-mice,' said Burglar with a grin. 'Reckoned I'd make a packet. But if it belongs to Rufus . . .' He opened his pack. At once, an angry red light blazed out. 'Cor, look at that! It weren't doin' that when I nicked it.' He reached in a paw, shot into the air, turned a somersault, and landed on his back. 'Ow! It hit me!'

'Serves you right for nickin' it,' said Finn.

Rufus helped Burglar to his feet. Then, as the others watched nervously, he gently lifted out the Crown. At once, the angry gleam faded. 'Yes! This is it! Well done, Burglar. Saraband will have a shock when he finds it has vanished.'

'No doubt,' said Finn thoughtfully. 'But how come *you* didn't get a shock when you picked it up?'

'I don't know. But . . . I found the other Treasures. Maybe I was meant to find this Treasure, too.'

Finn reckoned there was more to it than that. But he kept his thoughts to himself.

The Crown was still as tarnished as when Rufus had first seen it but, deep inside the ruby, a tiny heart was beating. The mice gazed in awe, sensing its power.

Carefully, Rufus stowed it in his pack. 'What will you do now, Finn?'

'Return to Aramon. Will you come?'

'No. Now that we have the Treasures, we must find the eagles. The poem is quite clear on that: '. . . *go with the Treasures and seek for the eagles. The King shall arise and the rats be destroyed.*'

'But without the Treasures, the city may fall!'

'Perhaps. But you cannot think only of Aramon; you must think of all Carminel. Without the eagles, final victory is impossible. Hold the city as long as you can but, if it falls, get out with as many mice as possible. Go west, to the Castle in the Marshes. I will find you there – and, with the eagles, we will drive out the rats for ever.'

Finn was a master of strategy. No one had ever questioned him before. He opened his mouth to argue, but the look in Rufus's eyes made him shut it again.

'Better do as he says, Boss,' murmured Burglar.

Finn sighed. 'All right. But do you know where you're going?'

'The mountains. We'd be grateful for any help you can give.'

'Well now, in the days of my famous ancestor, Conal,' said Finn, 'the eagles lived in Gideon's Castle in the High Collada Mountains. Gideon's tribe were a fierce, proud breed o' mice. They, and the eagles, may still be there. Since you have the Treasures, mice and eagles will surely agree to fight for us again. Neither rats nor Red Kites will stand against an eagle-charge. But it's a long, dangerous journey. We'll give you enough food for a week and you can stock up at Gideon's old tower. There's plenty of firewood there, too.'

Rufus nodded. 'It's near the moles' city. Morganna told us about it. And after that?'

'Go north. Take food and weapons from the tower, and some warm clothing. Find the eagles. And may the Lord o' Light protect you!'

The fire was out. Rufus and Elana, their packs stuffed with food, were preparing to leave, when a mouse hurried up the path. 'Boss! The rats are up to somethink. They're loading their guns, an' cleanin' their weapons – an' there's a crowd of 'em comin' into the forest! We'd better scarper!'

'Right!' Finn pointed north. 'There's your path, and here's my spare pistol and some ammo – just in case. Good luck!'

With a wave to their new friends, Rufus and Elana set off up the track. The eastern sky was tinged with pink; the great star had faded. In the distance, a bugle blared from the rats' camp.

'You hear that?' said Finn. 'That's action stations. Looks like Saraband's going to attack the city sooner than we thought. Let's go!'

20 Dawn Attack

'Good work, Finn! Both siege-guns wrecked!' From the roof of the Great Fortress, Cardinal Odo was studying the rats' siege-line through his telescope. 'But what are they up to now?'

Finn could plainly see a horde of rats emerging from the forest, carrying tall, slender trees. They began hacking off the branches, taking care to leave short stumps sticking out all the way to the top of each trunk.

'They're making ladders, sir. But I don't think they'll risk an attack in broad daylight. Dawn tomorrow's my guess, so we'd better get ready.'

'You are right. Anything else to report?'

Finn told the Cardinal all about his meeting with Rufus and Elana. 'I wanted them to bring the Treasures here. But Rufus insisted on finding the eagles first. It's strange, sir; Rufus doesn't look like a slave, or talk like one. Carries himself like a General . . . *And I found myself obeyin' his orders*!'

'I'm looking forward to meeting Rufus. He was right to seek the eagles. We must try and hold the city until they come! And you say that only Rufus was able to touch the Crown? I must tell McCrumb about that. He knows more about the Treasures than I do. Finn, I'm making you Captain of Aramon, so get busy and organize our defences!'

As the word spread, soldiers and citizens threw themselves into preparations for the big attack. Fear was mixed with relief that the waiting was nearly over. Barricades of boxes, tables and chairs sprang up in every street in case the city itself became a battleground. While mice cleaned their weapons, delicious smells rose from the houses as the mouse-wives cooked the last of the food. 'Let all mice eat well tonight,' said Odo cheerfully. 'We cannot fight on empty bellies!'

Finn was leaving nothing to chance. Relays of

mice were organized to carry ammunition up to the walls; buckets of water were placed outside every house in case of fire, and all children were taken to the Great Cathedral and placed under the care of old Bishop Sigmond and the good priests of the Lord of Light. Finn even found time to visit Silence, who was prowling restlessly around the hospital in the Great Fortress. His arm was paralyzed, but the wound was healing well. He had no intention of staying out of the battle.

'Dead-Eye's in charge at the North Gate,' said Finn. 'Burglar's at the West Gate. Yes, I know,' he added, as Silence pulled a face. 'The West Gate's the weak spot, and it's where Saraband will attack hardest. Burglar will just have to take his chance. At least you're well out of it.'

Silence scowled ferociously. He did not want to be out of it.

Finn laughed. 'All right! Look, I've brought you a brace of pistols. Can you shoot with your left paw?'

Silence nodded eagerly, then pointed through the window, and put on a plaintive expression.

'No! I want you here. Look after the other wounded. I'll be sending weapons in for them later. If the rats get into the Fortress, I'll be relyin' on you to get these mice to safety. So don't argue!'

Finn's command post was a tavern on the corner of the Cathedral Square. As he walked past the city walls in the gathering dusk, mice on the battlements waved and called greetings to him. In the shadow of the walls, more mice were crouching round their watch fires. Finn stopped to talk to them, telling them jokes, making them laugh, and marvelling at their cheerful courage.

As darkness fell, a tense silence settled over the city. Finn was restless. Around midnight, he left his command post and headed for the North Gate, where he found Dead-Eye and his section tense and anxious.

'Can't see a ruddy thing,' muttered Dead-Eye. 'No stars. The rats have put out their fires. If you ask me, the devils are up to something. We could do with Silence up here now. D'you reckon Rufus'll make it in time?'

Finn sighed. 'I doubt it. But we'll hold 'em off as long as we can! I'll go and see how Burglar is. Good luck! Keep careful watch!'

Above the West Gate, Burglar's mice were crouching like statues, staring fixedly into the darkness. Far away, an owl hooted to its mate, but no other sound broke the deathly silence, save the Cathedral clock, tolling the hours.

'Four o'clock,' muttered Burglar. He knew the Gate's weakness and was not looking forward to the morning. 'Soon be dawn. You get back to HQ, Boss. We'll be all right.'

But Finn was feeling uneasy. Why had the rats put out their fires? 'I'll stay a little longer . . . *What was that*?' He leaned over the battlements, listening intently. Again he heard it – a faint rustling, drawing nearer . . . and nearer . . . A gentle breeze awoke and whispered round the walls. Finn sniffed. '*Rats*!'

Now, in the first glimmer of dawn, he could see hunched shapes on the ground, at no great distance from the Gate. The rats were there, covered by their cloaks. The rustling he had heard was their ladders. Far behind them loomed the menacing shape of another siege-gun.

Finn's yell shattered the silence. 'Get those rats! Fire!' But even as the mice shot a deadly volley, the siege-gun roared. A massive round-shot struck the old timber Gate. It shuddered, but held. Now, from all round the outside of the city, siege-guns thundered. But only two were firing at the Gates. The others were hurling their shots over the walls, or hammering the Great Fortress. As the shots screamed over the battlements, the rats made a dash

138

for the walls, raised their ladders and scrambled up.

The mice were ready for them. They waited until the rats were almost at the top, then shoved hard at the ladders with their rifle-butts. Rats screamed as they toppled to the ground and fled as the defenders opened fire. But another forest of ladders appeared, and once more the mice heaved and strained to push them down.

At the third shot, the old timbers of the West Gate groaned. Instantly, a horde of rats charged. 'Fire!' yelled Burglar, and the rats were stopped in their tracks. 'I must get back to HQ,' said Finn. 'I'll send you reinforcements. Good luck!'

As Finn hurried through the streets, he heard the roar of battle breaking out all along the walls. The mice were yelling like furies, hurling the ladders down, and firing steadily on the rats.

A shout went up as Cardinal Odo appeared. Wearing a soldier's clothing of buff-coat, breeches and boots, and followed by the faithful McCrumb, he strode along the ramparts, praising, encouraging, organizing help for the wounded. He brandished his great club at the rats, daring them to enter his city.

Still the guns thundered, and red-hot cannon-balls crashed into the tightly-packed houses. A steady stream of messengers was coming and going in the Cathedral Square, as Finn calmly gave his orders. The situation at the West Gate worried him, but at least, he thought, the Great Fortress should hold out.

But, unknown to Finn, at that very moment the Great Fortress was in deadly peril.

21 The Fight for the Fortress

'*Gobtooth*!'

Saraband was furious. The attack had been going on for hours and still the walls held out. Gobtooth had better find another way in.

'Take some reliable rats, not those idiots Nym and Skillet, and go round to the east side of the Fortress. See if you can find an unguarded sewer – anything!'

Calling for two of his rats, Gobtooth hastened to

the end of one of the long trenches below the Fortress. The rats crouched in the mud beside their guns, while Gobtooth peeped cautiously over the top. To his left, the Fortress wall curved away, undefended, as far as Gobtooth could see. All the mice's attention was on the rats in the trench who were loading and firing the siege-gun.

'Aim higher!' snapped Gobtooth. 'Keep their heads down while we get out of here!'

The gunners obeyed and the defenders ducked as a shot smashed against the parapet.

'Now!' Gobtooth and his rats scrambled out and pelted to the unprotected side of the Fortress. There the ground fell steeply away from the towering wall. The rats almost slipped, but they clung to the stone-work, inching along until –

'Captain! Look! A door, low in the wall, almost invisible.'

'The postern gate,' said Gobtooth. 'So small, but big enough for us! You two – back to Saraband. Tell him to send three companies of warriors and any-thing that'll burn. We'll soon have this little door down.'

'Come on, Silence! Let's get out of here and sort them rats out!'

Corporal Draggletail and the other wounded mice of the Dirty Squad were tired of skulking in the hospital. They could hear shots thudding against the Fortress, and were desperate to join the battle. So was Silence. But Finn had ordered him to stay put unless the rats broke in, so he smiled and shook his head. As the wounded mice groaned, a young officer, gasping for breath, tumbled into the room.

'Silence! We've spotted some rats heading for the postern gate. Going to break in. No mice available – all up on the roof – can you –?'

'Yes!' roared Draggletail. Silence nodded eagerly. The mice hastily tightened their bandages, picked up their crutches, snatched up their rifles and hobbled out of the hospital, down to the Great Hall.

Silence led them along the passage towards the postern gate. But they had not gone far when the acrid stench of burning rags set their whiskers twitching; smoke was billowing round the door.

Raising his good arm, Silence made three chopping movements. The soldiers understood. Hastily, they formed three ranks – one crouching, one kneeling, one standing. Coughing and choking on the smoke, the little company cocked their rifles and waited.

Outside, the rats were howling with excitement,

calling on the Sable Lord to help them. Suddenly, the ancient timbers vanished behind a wall of flame. Narrowing his eyes against the blinding smoke, Silence could see the rats cowering from the blazing door. He signalled to the front rank. The narrow passage echoed to the crash of gunfire, and the rats screamed and vanished. But as the door crumbled to a heap of glowing ash, first one rat then another leapt across and charged down the passage. They were cut down as the second rank fired.

But now the rats were flooding in. Silence gave the signal for one more volley. As the mice hastily reloaded, he signalled them back. Halting at the end of the passage, they fired a triple volley. Still the rats came on, screaming their battlecries, and Silence signalled his mice back across the Great Hall towards the doors.

As the rats poured in, the mice fired one more devastating volley before hobbling out into the courtyard, slamming the doors behind them.

'Boss! The rats are in the Fortress!'

'Draggletail! Is Silence all right?'

'Yeah! He an' the lads are fightin' a rearguard action outside the Fortress. The rats fired the postern gate. We tried to stop 'em, but there was too many, an' there's more of 'em pourin' in every minute!'

'Boss! Message from Dead-Eye. The North Gate's down. We're holdin' 'em back, but —'

'Boss! The West Gate's down. The rats are through! Burglar's fallin' back!'

'Captain Finn!' Cardinal Odo, his fur blackened with smoke, shouldered his way through, followed by McCrumb, who was bristling with pistols. 'The rats are in the city,' said Odo calmly. 'What do you advise?'

Finn thought quickly. 'Sir, if the rats have taken both Gates and the Fortress, the city must fall. Will you go to the breach in the north wall? I'll order every mouse to make a fightin' retreat towards it. We'll get as many out as we can.'

'What then?'

'Rufus said to go west, to the Castle in the Marshes. I think we should do as he said, for it's there he'll look for us when he has the eagles.'

As the Cardinal and McCrumb hurried away, Finn turned to the messengers. 'It's all right, lads. Keep calm. Tell Dead-Eye, Burglar and Silence to hold them off as long as they can. And pass the word to the mice on the walls that they must keep the rats away from the breach!'

*

A rat panted up to Saraband. 'My lord! Gobtooth's taken the Fortress and both Gates are down!'

Saraband flung out his paws and yelled with glee. The city was his! 'Excellent! Halt the attack on the wall! Every warrior on the right to attack through the West Gate; those in the centre go for the North Gate, and the left wing to the Fortress!'

Yelling for the Red Kites to take over the attack on the walls, Saraband hurried off to join the attack on the Great Fortress. Already, he pictured his warriors acclaiming him King.

Still the siege-guns thundered, but now the rats were firing heated round-shot, and house after house exploded in flames. Sparks flew on a rising wind until whole districts were ablaze, and the terrified cry arose: 'Wildfire!'

Burglar, Dead-Eye and Silence had fought their way to the breach. Here, the houses were as yet unharmed. Using them as cover, the mice kept up a deadly fire upon the advancing rats, while Odo and McCrumb urged the females, and those mice too old to fight, over the breach. Outside the walls, the rats were swarming towards the Gates and the Fortress, and the way to safety would soon be clear.

Realizing that their enemies were leaving them alone, the mice on the battlements turned their rifles on the rats inside the city. Packed in the narrow streets, the warriors soon found themselves in a death-trap. 'Back!' they screamed but it was no use, for more rats were pouring through the Gates. For a moment, Finn wondered whether the enemy had brought about their own destruction.

But Red Kites were diving on the ramparts. Once again, the mice found themselves fighting for their lives. 'Hold them!' yelled Finn. Mice were steadily climbing the slope of rubble. Gradually, Finn's own mice were retreating, closer to the breach. Other soldiers were falling back along the walls, desperately defending themselves against the Red Kites.

Finn knew the end was near. He was about to call out to Odo to leave the city and save himself, when he suddenly remembered the children. They were still in the Cathedral! 'Burglar! Dead-Eye! Follow me!'

To either side, the streets were full of rats. But they dashed down a narrow lane and had just reached the end, when the whole street in front of them vanished in a wall of flame.

22 'The Last Fight!'

Reeling back from the burning houses, the mice darted up a side-turning and flung themselves flat as a flight of bullets whistled over their heads. 'Charge!' yelled Finn, and they dashed for the barricade, leapt to the top, fired their pistols, then hacked their way clear, sprinting off down the street before the rats knew what had hit them.

The mice pelted down side streets and back alleys, seeing the pall of smoke spreading over the city. At last, they reached the Cathedral Square, and saw a huddle of children with Bishop Sigmond of

Aramon and a group of black-robed priests, looking almost as terrified as their charges. Finn panted up to the Bishop. 'Are they all here, sir?'

'Oh, dear me, I do hope so, yes, I certainly hope so,' quavered the old mouse, 'though you never can tell with children. They keep running off, you know. But I think they're all here.'

'No, we ain't!' called a young mouse, pointing at the Cathedral. 'Snout's still in there!'

'I'll go,' said Burglar.

The Great Cathedral was cold and dark. At first, Burglar could see nothing but deep shadows; then, peering up to where a solitary candle still burnt on the high altar, he spotted a small figure sitting on the floor, calmly eating a loaf of holy bread. Burglar snatched it from him and replaced it on the altar. 'You shouldn't be eatin' that!'

'Why not? I'm 'ungry!'

'Look – nickin' bread when you're 'ungry is one fing. Nickin' 'oly bread's another.'

'Can't see why – bread's bread, ain't it?'

Burglar had no time to argue. Gripping the little mouse's paw he hauled him off, still protesting, down the aisle.

'Your name Snout?'

'Yeah.'

'Why do they call you that?'

'Got a long snout, ain't I? You goin' to make somefink of it?'

Burglar grinned. 'I might! But now we're goin' to find your mum, and get you an' the others out of here.'

'Ain't got no mum. Nor dad. Me an' my mates live on the streets – don't 'ave to go to school!'

Blimey, thought Burglar, just like I used to be!

Outside, Finn was organizing the children into groups, each under the protection of a priest. 'I'll lead!' he called, as Burglar and Snout emerged from the Cathedral. 'Dead-Eye, look after the middle groups. Burglar, you cover the rear.'

'Burglar?' squeaked Snout. 'You're one of the Dirty Squad, ain't ya?'

Burglar grinned down at him. 'Yeah! You goin' to make somefink of it?'

Snout smiled back, and gripped Burglar's paw more tightly. 'I might!'

As they hurried through the streets, the dark clouds opened and more snow began to fall. The sound of firing grew louder, and the smell of gunpowder lay heavy on the air. As they approached the final turning, Finn signalled the children to stop while he ran to the corner. He peeped round. The street was full of rats. 'Can't go down there,' he told the Bishop. 'Wait here. I'll see if there's another way through.'

But the fighting had spread, until every house was a fortress, every street a battleground. Several fires were blazing unchecked, and the snowflakes, falling through the smoke, looked like tiny black spiders.

Finn ran back. 'We're stuck. Any ideas, Burglar?'

'No, Boss, but young Snout reckons he knows a way through.'

'Well, Snout?'

'Are you Captain Finn?' asked Snout, his eyes wide.

'Yes, and if you've got any ideas, let's hear 'em.'

'Cor! Can I join the Dirty Squad?'

Finn smiled at the scruffy little mouse. 'Get us out of here, and I'll make you a Section Leader!'

Grinning from ear to ear, Snout drew himself up and saluted. 'Right, Boss! Follow me!' He led them back to the next street and halted beside an iron grating in the gutter. 'Down there. That's the sewers. It pongs a bit, but it'll take us to the breach.'

Snout put his paws in his mouth and whistled. Several ragged little mice ran up to him. 'Get that cover up!' ordered Snout. 'An' be quick about it!

We're in the Dirty Squad now – an' I'm a Section Leader!'

The shallow stream flowed towards a distant glimmer of light. To either side, gaping pipes added a constant dribble of black, sludgy water. Underfoot, the way was squashy, though mercifully invisible. Snout was leading, followed by his gang, all gleefully kicking the mucky water over one another.

'Will you stop that?' yelled Finn. He was used to nasty smells, but preferred not to have his clothing soused in them.

At last, Snout reached the end of the tunnel and, as he and his gang swarmed up the ladder and raised the grating, the sound of firing, muffled by the sewer, once more echoed in their ears.

Finn scrambled out. Behind him, through the falling snow, mice were pouring up the slope of rubble. At the top, Odo and McCrumb were waving and cheering them on. But the bullets were singing around them, for the defence of the city had shrunk to a tight semicircle in front of the breach. Only the Dirty Squad and a company of soldiers from the walls remained to keep the rats at bay. Their rank stench, mingled with the smell of burning and the stink of powder, assaulted Finn's whiskers as the rats began to advance across a

152

desolation of burnt-out houses.

Several mice were out of ammunition. With drawn swords, they awaited the final assault.

Silence came up, grinning and wrinkling his snout. 'Yes, I know,' said Finn. 'I stink. We all do, so you may as well get used to it. Now, back in the line! Dead-Eye, go with him. Burglar, get these priests and kids away and tell the Cardinal to go too. And don't argue! I'm givin' you an order!'

'Can't we stay an' fight?' asked Snout. This was just what Burglar wanted to do, but he could see that the little mouse and his gang were terrified, in spite of Snout's brave words. All the youngsters were clustering round Burglar, too proud to ask, but begging him with their eyes to lead them away from the doomed city.

'See you later, then, Boss,' muttered Burglar, convinced that he would never see Finn or his comrades again. He turned away and helped old Bishop Sigmond up the slippery slope, the children slithering and stumbling after him. 'Finn says it's time to go, sir,' he called to the Cardinal.

'Very well,' said Odo. 'Finn! Come back now!'

'Och, he'll no' hear ye,' grumbled McCrumb. 'I'll go an' tell him.' As he tottered down the slope, McCrumb drew his pistols.

'McCrumb!' yelled the Cardinal. 'Come back!'

McCrumb pretended not to hear. Proudly, he took his place in the line, and the Dirty Squad welcomed him.

The rats stopped firing. They drew their swords, and greedily licked their lips.

Finn smiled at his mice. 'The last fight, lads. Let's make it a good one. CHARGE!'

With a blood-curdling yell, they hurled themselves upon the rats. The last Burglar saw of them, they were fighting valiantly in the midst of their enemies. Then, sick at heart, he followed Snout and the Cardinal down the slope and out on to the snowy plains. Far ahead, like a dark smear, but already vanishing into the white mist, the mice of Aramon trudged wearily away.

In the Great Hall of the Mouse-Kind, King Saraband sat alone. Through the tall windows came raucous shouts, and flames flickered against the darkening sky as the warriors looted and burnt. Saraband's face was a mask of fury. His conquest of the city, even the great shout of acclamation as his warriors hailed him as their King, had given him no pleasure. For the Crown had vanished, and he was no true King of Carminel without it.

Out of the shadows, a stooping figure was limping towards him. It was Morvan, the High Priest, his black robe embroidered with silver crescent moons, the tails of long-dead rats dangling from his staff.

'Well?' snapped Saraband. 'Where is the little beast?'

'You mean Rufus?' Morvan's voice was like a creaking hinge.

Saraband snarled. 'Of course I do. The Crown was in my tent and if that accursed slave hasn't stolen it, I don't know who has.' Saraband sank his voice to a whisper. 'You have the Sight. Tell me where to find Rufus.'

Gradually, the priest's eyes lost focus, as if he were searching far beyond the Fortress. 'I see mountains . . . and two mice. I see the Crown . . . and a jewelled Sword –'

'What? You mean that damned slave has the Sword as well? Rubbish! The poem was clear as daylight. It's here, under our feet. I've had teams of rats digging since we got here. You old fool! I tell you, Rufus is hiding in the city and I want to know where!'

The priest's eyes glittered angrily. 'Do you dare to insult me, Saraband? I am telling you the truth. Ignore me at your peril.'

Saraband hesitated. 'Maybe you're right. But wherever Rufus is, I'll find him. Now I want to know the future. Will I live, and rule this land?'

'You may not like what you hear.'

'I'll risk that. Just tell me!'

'You will rule in the Mouse-Lord's Hall,
Until by daylight stars shall fall;
And darkness hide the morning skies,
And from the west the sun shall rise.'

Saraband sprang to his feet, quivering with excitement. 'Now, that's more like it! Stars falling by day, darkness at noon, the sun rising in the west? Why, none of that can possibly happen!'

'It might.'

'Nonsense! Go and have a rest. You look exhausted. Tiring business, foretelling the future.'

Morvan shrugged. 'Very well. But don't say I didn't warn you.'

As the High Priest limped away, Saraband sent for Gobtooth. 'Well, have you found it?' he asked cheerfully.

Gobtooth brushed the dirt from his clothes. 'No. And we can't dig any more. It's too dark down there, and the lads want their share of the plunder.'

Saraband scowled. 'You'll dig till I tell you to stop. The Sword is here, you brainless fool, and you're going to find it!'

Wearily, Gobtooth turned away. He was just passing through the shadowed doorway, when Saraband called, 'Wait! Morvan reckons Rufus and the Sword are up in the mountains. I think he's wrong but we might as well make certain. Send a couple of Red Kites out at dawn. And keep digging!'

Part Four

Eagles
over
Carminel

23 Ghosts

'We're lost,' said Rufus.

The mice were exhausted. All day, they had tramped across fields and moors, searching for the old tower. Now, as they halted at the edge of a wood, Elana sank to the ground. The snow felt soft to her aching limbs and she longed for sleep.

'Can't we rest for a while?'

'No! If we fall asleep, we're done for. Come on. We must keep going . . . Elana! Look! There, above the wood! Can't you see it?'

Elana could see nothing: only the swirling snow

and the gaunt, dark trees. But Rufus had caught a glimpse of a huge bird, its wings beating slowly. Small figures were clinging to its back.

'Come on. Let's follow it.' Gripping Elana's paw, he hauled her up and she staggered after him into the wood.

Rufus was running, tripping over fallen branches, stumbling over tree-stumps half-submerged by snow, but never losing sight of the great eagle. At last, bruised, battered and bleeding, the mice panted out of the wood. On top of a low hill stood a tall, circular tower. Rufus watched as the eagle landed in a flurry of snow, and saw mice scrambling from its back. One of them flung open the door and waited while the others stumbled inside. Finally, the eagle lowered its head and followed them in, and the door slammed shut.

'Come on, Elana!' he cried.

Dumb with cold and misery, Elana followed him up the slope. She had no idea what Rufus was talking about.

Pushing open the door, Rufus strode in. He was expecting a roaring fire, bright candles, food and drink and the company of mice. But the room was dark, cold, and empty. Through the unglazed windows, flurries of snow blew in and settled on the icy stone floor. 'Where are they? Perhaps they've gone upstairs!'

'Oh, Rufus!' Elana had sunk to the floor. 'You're overtired. You're seeing things that don't exist! Please . . . just light a fire before we freeze to death!'

Rufus crossed to the huge fireplace, where a pile of logs lay ready, and fumbled in his pack for his tinderbox. Was he going mad?

Elana dragged herself over to the comforting blaze. 'Food,' she murmured. 'Finn said there was – *what was that*?'

A faint scrabbling noise . . . from an upstairs room. Rufus drew his pistol. 'Stay here!'

The stairs spiralled upwards into utter darkness. Rufus climbed until he sensed he was in another large room. Over by the wall, he could hear some-one breathing. 'Come here!' he commanded.

'Rufus?'

'*Wiglaff*!'

Rufus had found the entrance to the cellar. Huge wooden crates held an abundance of winter vege-tables, sweet-smelling herbs hung in bunches, and in a corner stood several racks of elderflower and blackberry wine.

While Elana cooked a stew, Rufus and Wiglaff

emptied two bottles of wine into a saucepan, added cinammon and cloves, and hung it on a hook over the fire. Delicious smells filled the room, and the mice settled down to their first hot meal for days. Wiglaff had brought his own supply of worms, but he accepted a goblet of spiced wine.

After the meal, the three friends gathered round the fire. Rufus showed Wiglaff the Crown, and told him how Burglar had stolen it from Saraband's tent. The little mole gazed in awe at the softly gleaming ruby. 'It's wonderful . . . and now you're off to find the eagles.'

'Yes, but I've seen one already,' said Rufus, with a defiant look at Elana. 'It was carrying mice. Elana thinks it was an illusion. Do you?'

'No,' said Wiglaff, 'because I've seen it too.'

'What?' squeaked Elana.

'I've seen it. Lots of times. But not in the way Rufus saw it. Come with me and bring some candles!'

Wiglaff led the way upstairs. As they stepped into the upper room, the mice gasped in wonder.

Glowing colours leapt from the walls. As the candle-flames steadied, Rufus and Elana realized that they were looking at a series of pictures, painted directly on to the plaster. So lifelike were the figures,

164

that Rufus felt he had only to call out and they would step into the room.

Wiglaff pointed to the first picture. 'There's your eagle! Her name was Galliard and she always carried Lord Gideon. And in the next picture, she's landing outside this tower, and the mice are climbing down. You can almost see them shivering. Now they're inside, by the fire, just as you imagined they were.'

'Who painted these?' asked Rufus.

'My great-great-grandmother,' said Wiglaff proudly. 'I told you Gideon was a friend of the Mould-Warp, and she knew him well. See that tall mouse, opening the door? That's Gideon!'

Rufus stared at the legendary Eagle Warrior. Although he had only seen Gideon for a split second, on that terrifying day in the moles' city, he recognized him at once. Rufus smiled, and the kindly eyes in the painting seemed to smile back.

'Look! That's Finn!' Elana was pointing to a thin, wiry mouse, with a merry twinkle in his eyes. 'But it can't be!'

'That's Conal,' explained Wiglaff, 'Gideon's second-in-command and a mighty fighter. You told me he was Finn's ancestor.'

'Who's that?' Elana had spotted a small, rather shy-looking mouse.

'Dabo. He once saved Gideon's life, but was so sorely wounded that Gideon flew him to the Island of Peace, where he was healed by the Lord of Light.'

Rufus shook his head in wonder. Then he spotted another figure, standing a little apart from the others. 'And that?'

'Ah, that's Armand, Prince of Carminel. Gideon and his friends had just rescued him from the clutches of his enemies. They brought him here for safety. Later, he became King, but in his son's reign, the rats invaded. The King's only son was slain at the Battle of Collada River.'

As Rufus stared at the young Prince Armand, the colours seemed to glow more vibrantly. Suddenly, Rufus saw the Crown, gleaming brightly above the little mouse's head. Behind the painted figure appeared another: a beautiful young mouse, in a long dress, and round her neck hung a silver locket.

'Rufus!' Elana's voice seemed to come from a long way off. 'Are you all right?'

Rufus shook his head. The Crown and the beautiful mouse vanished. He stared at the painting of Prince Armand, wondering why he looked so familiar. He shivered suddenly and turned abruptly from the pictures. 'I'm all right. Let's go down. It's cold up here.'

They returned to the fireside. 'I often come to look at the pictures,' said Wiglaff. 'I know all the stories about Gideon. His memory is kept alive in our city. What you saw earlier, Rufus, really happened. But it was a long time ago.'

'You mean – they were ghosts?' whispered Elana.

'Yes. But friendly ones. They wouldn't have harmed you.'

Wiglaff and Rufus slept. But Elana lay awake, staring into the embers. At last she took a candle, and tip-toed upstairs. In the flickering flame, the eagle seemed to be moving. Elana could almost hear the beating of ghostly wings and the eyes of the painted mice were watching her.

She looked at the picture of young Prince Armand. The great dark eyes were wistful, almost as if he were seeing into the future. She looked more closely at the strong, rather stocky figure, the handsome head and the black fur, with its curious reddish tinge.

It might have been a picture of Rufus.

24 Terror on the Mountain

Wiglaff had wanted to come with them. But Rufus pointed out that worms would be hard to find in the mountains, so Wiglaff reluctantly agreed to stay behind.

Elana and Rufus set off at dawn. Wiglaff waved until they were out of sight. Then, with a sigh, he trotted off into the woods, heading for one of the many secret entrances to the moles' city. Looking back, he could just make out a pale blur – the High

Collada Mountains, floating ghost-like above the dawn mist. He wondered whether he would ever see his friends again.

The path was steep, and for a long time the mice climbed in silence. Elana was full of the picture of Prince Armand. She was wondering how to tell Rufus what was in her mind, when the track levelled out, and there before them were the mountains. Rocky crags, their snow-clad slopes gleaming blue in the sunlight; glittering ice-pinnacles, stabbing the sky and, at the end of the mist-shrouded valley that lay below them, towering peaks that rose and fell in waves like a silver ocean.

The path had dwindled to a narrow ledge, the mountain on one side, an endless drop on the other. The mice were struggling to stay upright, for a bitter wind was buffeting against them, numbing their faces with its icy breath. But, just ahead, the track passed beneath a rocky overhang, which Rufus thought might provide some shelter. Hugging the mountainside, they crept along until they reached the canopy of rock. Beneath it, the track widened into a small cave. 'Food!' declared Rufus.

Huddled in the cave, they munched apples and sipped cider. Elana's thoughts returned to the picture. 'Rufus . . . That line in the poem: *The King*

169

shall arise and the rats be destroyed. Who do you suppose the King might be?'

'I don't know. Could be anybody. A noble-mouse, in a fine mansion in Aramon, or a poor one. After all, the Lord of Light was born the son of a village baker!'

'Maybe it's Finn. Or Burglar!'

Rufus laughed. 'Not Burglar! Remember what happened when he tried to touch the Crown?'

'Perhaps it's Cardinal Odo.'

'Oh, no! No Cardinal can become King.'

Elana was surprised. 'Why not?'

Rufus looked puzzled. 'I don't know why I said that. I just know it's true.'

Elana was watching him closely. 'Rufus, what are you thinking about?'

'Oh . . . nothing.'

'Rufus! You really are infuriating. You go wandering off into your mind, and when I ask you what you are thinking about, you say, "oh, nothing"!'

'Sorry. If you must know, I was thinking about that picture of Prince Armand.' Abruptly, Rufus stood up and walked to the lip of the precipice. Staring down through the thinning mist, he saw a distant silver thread meandering across the valley floor. Moodily, he kicked a stone over the edge and watched it fall until it was out of sight.

'You don't have to tell me if you don't want to,' said Elana.

'It's not that! I do want to tell you . . . I can't remember much about my father, but Mother often told me about him. His name was Kylin. Under his command, the slaves rose up against the rats. They captured part of the castle. But when Zagora led a counter-attack and overpowered them, most surrendered. Zagora spared their lives; the rats needed slaves! My father and the other leaders fought on, but in the end, they were captured. Zagora had them put to death. He kept my father till last . . .'

Rufus gazed unseeing across the valley. 'He was a slave. But he was also a warrior, who inspired the other slaves to fight for freedom. My mother taught me all about him, and to love what he believed in. He had reddish-black fur. Like me. No other mouse I've ever seen has it except that mouse in the picture. Armand. He looked exactly like my father.'

'And like you! Oh, Rufus, don't you see? You must be descended from Armand! From the Kings of Carminel!'

Rufus felt as if a great wave were rolling towards

him. 'How could I be? You told me that the last Prince of Carminel was killed at the Battle of Collada River.'

'Suppose he wasn't! Suppose he was captured! The rats would've kept quiet about it in case our side had tried to rescue him. Why does the Crown glow so warmly when you're near it? And why are you the only one who can touch it?'

'If I am King – why didn't my mother tell me?'

'Perhaps she wanted you to find out for yourself. Perhaps you had to prove yourself. And you have! It's your destiny! You can't escape it!'

The wind died. The valley was still. It was as if Carminel were waiting for his decision. In his heart, he knew that Elana was right. But still he fought against it. As he stared out across the valley, a sudden movement caught his eye. A Red Kite was streaking towards them.

'*Look out*!' With drawn Sword, Rufus leapt to protect Elana. The Red Kite was almost upon him. But Rufus forced himself to hold his ground until the bird was hovering directly above. He swung the Sword and felt it strike against the creature's talons. The Red Kite screeched in pain. It wheeled away, circled the valley, gathering its strength, then darted for the ledge. It never saw the arrow that took it in the throat, just folded up in mid-air, and plummeted to the valley. Elana was trembling. She dropped her bow, and was turning back to the cave, when a second Red Kite swooped down, plucked her from the ledge and hovered, just out of reach. Rufus knew it was taunting him. When it felt like dropping Elana, it would. Then it would come for him.

With Elana in mortal peril, all Rufus's doubts vanished. Taking out the Crown, he held it high, feeling its power surging through him as he cried: 'Eagles! Eagles! I, Rufus, *King of Carminel*, command you!'

Scarlet light shot from the ruby, struck the opposite peaks, and splintered into a thousand glittering shards. Rufus raised the Crown higher – and the ruby's light turned to gold and soared into the sky.

Time hung suspended. But the Red Kite was slowly relaxing its grip on Elana.

Far below, shadows flitted across the valley. The Red Kite jerked up its head and screeched. Just above it hovered a great eagle.

The Red Kite fled. But three more eagles were streaking down the valley. The Red Kite was surrounded but, if it dropped Elana, it might still be able to out-fly its enemies. It opened its talons. Elana made a wild grab as she fell past the eagle flying directly below, but she was falling too quickly. She could see the silver stream getting wider and wider. Then it grew narrower again and she found herself soaring into the sky, as great wings bore her safely away.

25 Caval

Holding tightly to Rufus's waist, Elana scarcely noticed the biting wind as the great eagle flew into the sunset. Her whole body was glowing with the thought that Rufus had accepted his destiny so that he might save her life! She peeped down, and saw, far below, the broad shadows of the four eagles rippling across the flanks of the mountains. At last, the eagle slowed, turned, and began his descent in a series of lazy spirals. Rufus looked down – and gasped.

In a deep cleft in the mountains, a green valley

stretched into the distance. Above it rose a magnificent castle, perched on the edge of a rocky crag. Tall towers of an airy lightness soared from the keep, each one tipped by a curious, conical roof. In the valley, strange horned creatures were grazing. As the eagle spiralled lower, tiny figures looked up and waved. Rufus saw that they were mice.

As the eagle swooped to a graceful landing in the castle courtyard, more mice appeared; strange-looking, with long, thick fur under woollen caps, coats and leggings. A stout, motherly figure in cap and apron bustled up. 'Art reet then, lad? And thee, lass – happen th'art chilled t'marrow. Come along o'me; there's a warm fire and hot vittles for thee.'

Her accent was just recognizable as the language of Carminel, and though Rufus only understood about one word in three, there was no mistaking the old mouse's welcome. But before he followed her into the castle, he turned to the eagles. 'Thank you. I shall never forget what you have done for us.'

Slowly, the eagles lowered their heads; one by one, they gently touched their beaks to his out-stretched paw. A sudden silence fell over the courtyard. 'Nay,' whispered the old mouse. 'They've neer done that; no, not to Lord Caval himself.'

'Who is Lord Caval?' asked Elana.

'T' lord o' this castle. He's down in t' fields, but he'll be up directly, and anxious to see thee, I daresay.'

In the Great Hall, a fire was blazing. Its leaping flames glowed on the long, polished table that stretched almost the full length of the Hall, and brought out the colours of the tapestries lining the walls between the tall windows. Rufus and Elana basked in the warmth, munching hot rolls dipped in scalding soup.

At the sound of heavy boots ringing on the flagstones, the mice glanced up. A tall mouse, in a magnificent scarlet cloak, was striding down the Hall, followed by a crowd of mice.

'I am Lord Caval,' he said abruptly. 'Who are you?'

From his long, hooked snout and proud, dark eyes, it was clear that Caval was descended from Gideon himself. This was the climax of Rufus's quest. He had to persuade Caval to bring his eagles to the defence of Aramon. But Caval sounded so unfriendly that Rufus began to doubt. If he said he was King, would Caval believe him? Rufus looked down at his clothes; Dead-Eye's spare camouflage uniform, shabby and travel-stained, made him look more like a bandit than a King. He would not reveal his true self.

'This is Elana, daughter of Amren the priest. I am Rufus, son of Kylin. I was a slave in the Rats' Castle, but I escaped and, with Elana's help, I have found the Treasures of Carminel. Your eagles rescued us from Red Kites, sent by Saraband. We're very grateful.'

'My own eagle, Tarquin, slew the Red Kite. But as for the Treasures,' Caval said scornfully, 'what nonsense is this? Who is Saraband? And what were you doing in our mountains?'

Elana felt angry, but Rufus continued quietly: 'We were looking for you. Saraband is the rats' warlord, who at this moment is besieging Aramon. The city, and all Carminel, are in peril. We need you and your eagles. Will you come?'

Caval scowled. 'We live in peace here. I will not lead the eagles and my followers to war on the word of a slave!'

Rufus had no choice. He took a deep breath. 'Will you lead them to war on the word of a King?' Before the astonished Caval could reply, Rufus took out the Crown. It was tarnished no longer! Silver beams struck fire from its diamonds, and the ruby's beating heart poured out wave after wave of golden light.

'No mouse may hold the Crown except one!' cried Rufus. His eyes blazed and the mice flinched from the strength that radiated from him. 'I am the rightful King of Carminel! Your eagles obeyed my summons and I command you, Lord Caval, on your allegiance, to lead them to the defence of Aramon!'

Elana uncovered the glowing Chalice. Rufus drew the Sword, brandishing it so that its jewels glittered. Caval and his mice knelt, gazing in awe at Rufus and the Treasures.

'Only mice of the Royal House have reddish-black fur,' said Caval. 'The Crown is clearly yours. Long ago, my ancestor, Gideon, fought with that Sword in the defence of Carminel. I will not shame his memory by refusing your command. We will fight! And I rejoice that Carminel has a King again.'

'And I rejoice that you will help us to save Carminel!' Rufus offered the Sword to Caval. 'Take it! Use it to destroy the tyranny of Saraband!'

Caval rose and accepted the Sword. Again he knelt, and placed both his paws between Rufus's. 'I, Caval, Prince of Eagles, swear by all I hold dear, to serve and follow you and yours for the rest of my life.'

High above the castle, a great star was shining. Its light streamed through the windows, mingling with the golden light from the ruby. But only Rufus heard the familiar voice:

'By the strength of your will and your courage undaunted,
By steadfastly holding to that which is right,
You have the Treasures, now fight for your Kingdom!
Save it from darkness and bring it to light!'

That night, Rufus and Elana feasted in the Great Hall of Caval's castle. After the meal, a young mouse rose to his feet. He wore a cloak of white eagle feathers, a gold torque gleamed at his neck, and he carried a harp. As his paws struck the strings, the mice fell silent, and the bard began to sing of the famous adventures of Gideon, Conal, and the Eagle Warriors of old. His voice was strong and true, and the mice listened, enchanted.

As the song ended to wild applause, Caval beckoned to the singer. 'This is Bradwen, my brother: a fine bard – and a daring eagle rider!'

Bradwen was very different from his fierce elder brother. In a sparkling torrent of words, he told Rufus and Elana how excited the mice were feeling at the prospect of flying to Aramon, to pit their strength and that of their eagles against the rats.

Later that night, Rufus stood by the window of his bed chamber, gazing out over the moonlit mountains. Caval and his warriors had hailed him as their King; even the eagles had bowed to him. But could he really conquer Saraband? Despite Bradwen's confidence, Rufus suddenly felt terribly afraid.

After a long, cold flight, the Eagle Squadron landed by night on the desolate plain of Barrowdown, to the west of Aramon. Bradwen offered to go with Rufus to Aramon. Mounted on Juno, Bradwen's eagle, the two mice took off for the city.

Aramon was in darkness, but the Great Fortress was ablaze with light. Gently, Rufus touched Bradwen's shoulder and the mouse spoke softly to Juno, who began a slow, spiralling descent. Suddenly Rufus tensed. Dark shapes that he recognized only too clearly were hanging motionless from the battlements. 'Go back!' hissed Rufus. 'Red Kites!'

'Back, Juno!' said Bradwen, and the great eagle banked sharply and returned to Barrowdown.

'What now?' asked Caval.

'You and Bradwen come with me. Let's take a closer look.'

By dawn next morning, the three mice were lying on top of a low hill, with a clear view of the West Gate. Across the plain, country-mice were trudging towards Aramon, pulling carts laden with vegetables. The rats guarding the West Gate were letting them in. Other rats lined the walls. Red Kites were circling lazily overhead.

'A night attack?' suggested Bradwen.

'We'd be outnumbered,' replied Caval, 'but it might work if we achieved surprise! What do you think, Rufus?'

Rufus was thinking about Finn, and the rest of the Dirty Squad. Had they fled the city? Rufus doubted it. Were they dead, or prisoners? What had happened to all the other mice defending Aramon? Where was the Cardinal? 'We need information before we do anything,' he said. 'I must get into the city.'

'Too dangerous!' declared Caval.

'No,' said Rufus, an idea taking shape in his mind. 'The rats are letting those other mice in. Did you bring your harp, Bradwen?'

'Of course. We'll want some music for our victory feast. But why – ?'

'How would you like to play it . . . *for Saraband himself*?'

26 Spies

That afternoon, Rufus and Bradwen joined a party of country-mice plodding towards the West Gate. The farmers were tugging carts laden with cabbages and early potatoes to sell at the market.

'Them rats despise us,' a farmer told them, 'and give us poor prices – when they pay us at all. But we have to live somehow, and they've got to eat, so they let us in.'

Rufus was heavily cloaked and hooded, in case Saraband or one his warriors recognized him. But Bradwen, his cap decorated with eagle feathers, looked the very picture of a wandering minstrel.

'I am Lorenzo the Incomparable!' he announced as they arrived at the Gate. 'And this scruffy specimen is my assistant, Malodorus. We have journeyed far to bring music and song to the taverns of this famous city!'

Nym and Skillet, still out of favour with Saraband, were on guard duty. They had never met a minstrel before, and Bradwen's breezy personality suggested that his music would be much more entertaining than that of their own bards. 'Come on in,' said Nym. 'Now, the best taverns are down by the docks, and when you've finished there, come up to the Fortress. We could do with some fresh songs!'

Bradwen swept off his cap in a low bow. 'It will be a pleasure! I have a new song about the conquering rats and their glorious leader, Saraband!'

'I'd like to 'ear that, wouldn't you, Skills? I like a nice ballad, 'specially when it's about us!'

The country-mice were scowling, but they were far too scared of the rats to say anything. Bradwen ignored them and strutted boldly through the Gate.

'Have you really got a song about Saraband?' murmured Rufus, as they threaded their way through the streets towards the harbour.

'Two, actually,' replied Bradwen. 'But only one of them's fit for his ears. If he heard the other, we'd both finish up in the dungeons.'

Many houses still lay in ruins but, already, the mice who had remained in the city were rebuilding. In the Cathedral Square, bright with market-stalls, swaggering rats jostled the city-mice out of the way, poking and prodding at the fruit and vegetables, scooping up the pick of the crops. Some threw tiny coins in exchange; most simply helped themselves, cuffing any mouse brave enough to ask for payment. The smell of rat was everywhere. Bradwen sauntered along, his nose in the air, with 'Malodorus' shuffling humbly behind.

That evening, Bradwen sang at The Lord Saraband, an old dockside tavern in Vittles Lane. Rufus noticed that beneath the fresh paint, the old name was still visible: The Cardinal's Head. Clearly, the fat landlord, Pozzo, thought it best to keep in favour with the new ruler of Aramon.

In the crowded bar-parlour, the air was thick with tobacco smoke, and smelt foully of rats. Bradwen found a space by the fire, called loudly for silence, and ran his paws over his harp-strings. The rats gave a sarcastic cheer but, as the first notes rippled to the rafters, they fell silent and listened.

Bradwen improvized a song about a lonely rat, far from his loved ones and beset by enemies. Quietly at first, he sang of the warrior's longing for home; then, judging the moment perfectly, he shattered the mood with a harsh discord – now, his warrior was battling with savage foes and, of course, overcoming them all. With a flourish, Bradwen ended his ballad by revealing the name of his hero: Saraband!

The applause was deafening, and when Rufus went round with the hat, he was showered with gold. The rats gathered round Bradwen, clapping him on the back, and thrusting mugs of ale into his paws, but Pozzo, and the few mice drinking at the bar, scowled in disgust. If only we could tell them who we really are, thought Rufus sadly.

'You! Minstrel!' The rats fell silent. From a corner table, Gobtooth had spoken. 'Come to the Fortress tomorrow night. King Saraband is holding a great feast to celebrate our victory. He would like to hear your song; so would the rest of our comrades.'

With a wink at Rufus, Bradwen bowed low. 'My Lord – it will be an honour!'

The rats had gone. In the bar-parlour, the candles were burning low. Pozzo was stumping round, collecting empty beer mugs. He scowled at the two mice seated by the fire. 'You two – out!'

'We'd like to stay the night,' said Rufus.

Pozzo snorted. 'I don't let rooms to friends of the Rat-Kind!'

'What about their enemies?' asked Bradwen.

'That's different. But you ain't their enemies. On yer way!'

'Pozzo!' Rufus stood up and threw back his hood. As the firelight fell on his reddish-black fur, the landlord stared in astonishment. The scruffy, down-trodden Malodorus had vanished. In his place stood a mouse who looked like a King.

'Who are you?' he whispered.

'Not what we seem. I am Rufus, the rightful King of Carminel, and this is Bradwen, brother to Caval, Eagle Warrior.'

'Lord o' Light be praised! Welcome home, my Lord, and you too, sir! But – does this mean that the eagles have returned?'

'Yes. We cannot drive the rats from the city. But if we can lure them outside the walls, we'll stand a chance of beating them. But first we need soldiers. Tell me, what happened when the city fell? And what happened to Finn?'

*

'. . . so I don't know if Finn's alive. All the prisoners are held in the dungeons beneath the Great Fortress. There's sickness there already, but the rats don't care; word is, Saraband's starvin' them to death.'

'We must get them out,' said Bradwen. 'Any ideas, Rufus?'

For a long time, Rufus stared into the dying embers. At last, he smiled. 'Pozzo! This victory feast tomorrow night: who's supplying the wine?'

'Not me! They did ask but I said I didn't have enough.'

'Was that true?'

' 'Course not, my Lord! I've plenty of barrels, but not for those vermin!'

'Then, tomorrow, you will go to the Great Fortress and say you miscounted. Tell them they can have as many barrels as they want. And you, Bradwen, are going to be the star turn at Saraband's feast, so start writing some songs. You've got to sing as you've never sung before!'

27 Midnight Rescue

The following evening, a party of warriors arrived. 'We've come for the wine,' said Gobtooth.

'Come in, sirs!' cried Pozzo, all smiles. 'The barrels are in the cellar – thirty-six in all – and the finest wine in Aramon!'

'It'd better be!'

Night was falling as the final cartload disappeared round the corner. 'Now, sir,' said Pozzo, as Bradwen appeared in the bar-parlour, 'will you take some supper before you go?'

Bradwen was far too nervous to eat. But he

could not let the landlord see his fear. 'Just a mug of your best ale, Pozzo, and pour one for yourself. Here's to victory!'

Pozzo was feeling just as scared as Bradwen. 'Here's to you, sir! And the best of luck!'

When Bradwen arrived in the Great Hall, the victory feast was in full swing. The stench was ghastly, the noise deafening. As Bradwen strode in, an expectant hush descended. 'Lorenzo' was already famous, and the rats were anticipating a treat. With pounding heart, Bradwen approached the shadowed figure slouched on the throne at the far end of the Hall. Sweeping off his cap, the mouse made a low bow. 'Your majesty! I am most honoured –'

'Just sing!' snapped Saraband. 'And you'd better be good . . .'

Conquering his nervousness, Bradwen struck a chord and began his opening song. As his voice soared to the rafters, the rats fell under its spell.

As soon as he was sure that the rats had left the wine cellar, Rufus levered off the lid of his wine barrel. As it clattered to the floor, he clambered painfully out and collapsed. His limbs ached, and his head was reeling from the fumes. He longed to close his eyes and sleep for ever. But he dragged himself to the darkest corner of the cellar and slumped against the rough stonework until the cold air had cleared his throbbing head.

The door opened and two rats came in. Rufus ducked and froze while the rats rolled barrel after barrel out of the cellar. By the time they had gone, only a few barrels remained. Rufus listened intently. At last, through the thickness of the walls, he heard a distant, muffled bell tolling midnight. It was time!

In the Great Hall, Bradwen felt as if he had been singing for ever. After every song, the cheering rats would demand another and another. At last, as he came to the end of a rousing battle-song, Gobtooth appeared and thrust a mug of wine into his paw. 'Have a drink, minstrel! We'll hear more later.'

With a sigh of relief, Bradwen put down his harp, took off his feathered cap, and poured some wine down his aching throat. The Fortress clock tolled twelve. Down in the cellar, thought Bradwen, Rufus would be going into action.

Rufus eased open the cellar door and peeped out. All quiet. To the right, he could see steps, spiralling upwards. At the top, Pozzo had warned him, there would be a rat on guard. Moving softly, and gripping a crowbar, Rufus turned left and followed the dimly-lit passage until he arrived at the far end. Even before he reached the barred gate, Rufus's whiskers were twitching at the dreadful smell of sickness.

The great dungeon was unlit. Rufus made out a crowd of densely-packed bodies, snoring, snuffling, twitching in uneasy sleep. He reached through the bars and gently shook the nearest mouse. 'Wake up! I've come to get you out!'

The mouse opened his eyes. He was pitifully thin, but Rufus recognized him. 'Finn!'

'Who's that? Rufus, is it you? Lord o' Light! Did you bring the eagles?'

'Yes. They'll be here soon to fly you all to safety. Wake the others, while I work on this lock.'

At the far end of the dungeon, at the top of the spiral staircase, the jailer awoke. He stared blearily at his candle-clock. Past midnight? Stupid thing must be fast! But an officer would be along soon, so he'd better check on the prisoners. Reaching for his lantern, he heaved himself out of his comfy chair and headed for the top of the steps.

In the Great Hall, Bradwen was trying to make his drink last as long as possible. The racket was deafening. The rats were drunk; several fights had broken out. Gobtooth was lurching towards him. 'Gi's another song! We didn't bring you 'ere to drink all night! On yer feet, minstrel – sing!'

In the dungeon, the prisoners were awake. Sick,

wounded, they had given up all hope of rescue but, as Finn and Dead-Eye spread the news that Rufus and the eagles had come, a fever of excitement swept over them. Suddenly, Finn heard the jailer's footsteps clumping down the stairs. He must not hear the grinding of Rufus's crowbar attacking the lock. 'Sing!' he hissed. The mice opened their parched throats and launched into the song that every mouse in Aramon knew and loved: the rollicking marching song of the Dirty Squad.

'Once we fought in gutters, now we fight the
    common foe!
We are few and they are many –
Are we frightened? NO!
Scratching, kicking, biting, we will show them
    where to go!
We are the mice who will con-quer!
Look out – you rats – you'd better quake with
    fear!
Look out – you rats – the Dirty Squad is near!
We're the mice who'll bash you, smash you,
    boot you out of here!
YES! We're the mice who will con-quer!'

The jailer listened, then he shrugged, grinned sourly,

and returned to his comfy chair. The song reached its rousing climax and, with a splintering of metal, the dungeon door burst open.

28 Eagles Over Aramon

The sentry was standing with his back to the steps, listening to the faint sound of Bradwen's singing. He never heard Rufus, and slumped unconscious as the crowbar struck his head.

'Truss him up. Use your bootlaces, strips of clothing, anything!' As Finn and Dead-Eye swiftly obeyed, Rufus became aware of a mouse staring at him. He was dreadfully thin, and one paw hung uselessly at his side.

'That's Silence,' said Finn. 'He can't speak. He was wounded in the siege but he's still a great fighter. Silence, this is Rufus.'

The mouse smiled. Then, reaching out his left paw, he gently touched Rufus's head. 'Why did he do that?' asked Rufus.

Finn looked embarrassed. 'We told him about our meeting with you, on the night of the Lord of Light's Birthday, and how you were able to touch the Crown. He let us know, by signs, that he reckons . . . well, he reckons you're the King foretold in the old prophecy!'

'He's right,' said Rufus. 'I didn't believe it at first. But now I'm certain.'

Finn felt as if a great weight had been lifted from his shoulders. 'I thought so, sir! And not just because you alone were able to touch the Crown. You're the one we've been waiting for, no doubts about that! If I had my sword, I'd pledge it to your service!'

Rufus grinned. 'We'll get you another sword. But first, let's get out of here! According to Pozzo, there's a side door leading out into the courtyard . . .'

'There is, sir. This way!'

Barely able to see, they crept along the passage. Many of the mice were limping from wounds. All were weak from starvation, and several were so ill their comrades had to support them. But their hearts were beating joyfully as they followed their new King to freedom!

'Wait!' said Finn as they reached the door. 'Pass me your crowbar, sir. There'll be more than one sentry on the outer gate. This is a job for the Dirty Squad.'

Easing open the door, Finn and Dead-Eye melted into the darkness. Hugging the wall, they inched forward until they saw the gloomy outline of the main Gatehouse, where two sentries were blowing on their paws and stamping their feet.

'It just ain't fair,' said Nym. 'They're all up there enjoyin' themselves and we're stuck out 'ere in the cold!'

'Oh, leave off,' said Skillet. 'The relief'll be along soon. Honestly, the way you go on –'

'Here's the relief now,' said Nym, as two shadowy figures marched boldly towards them. 'Are we glad to see you! Here, just a minute! You ain't –'

Crack! As Nym collapsed, Finn and Dead-Eye hurled themselves at Skillet. Dead-Eye grabbed the rat's paw as he struggled to draw his pistol, while Finn thrust a gag into his mouth before throwing him to the ground where Dead-Eye swiftly bound the astonished rat's paws.

'Round the corner with 'em!' said Finn.

They dragged the rats out of sight. Returning to the Gate, they removed the bar and flung open the great doors.

Their weakness and hunger forgotten, the mice poured across the courtyard and followed Finn into the dark, silent city. Rufus remained behind to close the door and the Gate. Then, keeping in the shadow of the north wall, he hastened after the others towards the breach.

Bradwen played a final chord and stopped singing. No one was listening. The rats were all fighting drunk and the uproar was deafening. He glanced at Saraband; his eyes were closed. Tucking his harp under his arm, Bradwen forced himself to walk casually down the Hall. After side-stepping several fights, he reached the doors unnoticed. With a final glance over his shoulder, he slipped out into the courtyard. No sign of the sentries. Rufus had succeeded! Bradwen grinned with relief and was halfway to the Gate when – 'Minstrel! Stop!'

Bradwen swung round – and saw Saraband.

'Trying to sneak out, were you, Minstrel? But you cannot go yet. Here!'

Saraband was holding a little bag. Hearing the clink of coins, Bradwen almost collapsed with relief.

'Thank you, my Lord! I am most . . .' He reached up to sweep off his cap in a low bow. But his head was bare.

'Yours, I believe,' said Saraband, producing the cap from behind his back.

Bradwen silently cursed his carelessness. 'Yes, Lord King! How kind of you . . .'

Saraband was examining the cap. 'This feather is very handsome,' he said with a smile. 'Where did you get it?'

'Oh . . . I bought it. A long time ago, in the market, here in Aramon –'

'I think not,' purred Saraband, drawing his pistol. 'In my castle we have many like this, carefully preserved by the priests. So, where did you get this – eagle feather?'

Bradwen smiled. 'From my eagle. And one day, she and the rest of the Squadron will sweep you and your kind out of Carminel for ever!'

Turning swiftly on his heel, Bradwen gripped Saraband's paw, twisted it, and flung the rat over his shoulder. As Saraband flew across the courtyard, his pistol clattered to the ground. Bradwen picked it up, retrieved his cap, flung open the Gates and vanished.

As he sprinted along beneath the north wall, the

Great Cathedral clock tolled one. Suddenly, the stars were blotted out as a flight of eagles swooped over the battlements. Caval led the Squadron in a low, steep turn over the sleeping city, then back to the walls. Looking down, he saw eager paws reaching up as the whole eagle line hovered with wildly beating wings.

'Grab hold!' yelled the riders, and the mice leapt for the talons, gripped tightly, and were whisked away to the safety of Barrowdown. Again and again the eagles flew; several landed on top of the breach, where Rufus and Finn were helping the sick and wounded. These mice found themselves snuggling among soft feathers, then soaring into the sky and away!

'Nearly finished!' panted Rufus. 'One more flight should – Bradwen! I was wondering where you'd –'

But his grin of welcome faded as Bradwen gasped, 'Got caught – Saraband – better hurry – rats here soon!'

'Rats here now,' drawled Finn, as a horde of warriors came pounding up the lane.

The rats were so drunk that it had taken Saraband all this time to organize them. Eventually, his ranting and roaring had penetrated their fuddled brains. Grabbing their weapons, they reeled out of the Hall, tripping, sprawling, running the wrong way. 'Come on, you drunken imbeciles, the prisoners are escaping!' At last, they were running after him, following the north wall. 'There they are! Get them!'

As Saraband ran towards the breach, he wondered why the mice were not scampering away. He could see they were unarmed. He had been so long in the Great Hall that he had not seen the eagles. Now he did.

They came swooping out of the darkness, straight for the rats. Tarquin's open beak was like a sabre. Caval's great jewelled Sword seemed to take fire from the stars. Behind them, the rest of the warriors were screaming in excitement as their eagles wheeled into arrowhead formation for the charge.

The rats skidded to a halt, staring in horror. To their drink-sodden brains, these eagles looked like fiends from a nightmare. They turned and fled. 'Stand and fight, you damned cowards!' screamed Saraband, but the eagles were upon them and 'AAAARRRGGHH!' Forty pairs of talons flashed down, forty rats swung into the air. The eagles dropped them into the harbour, before returning for more.

Saraband found himself deserted. He had lost his

pistol but, as the eagles swooped again, he defiantly drew his sword. As Tarquin hovered over him, he yelled, 'You can't kill me! I bear a charmed life. Morvan said so!'

Tarquin's wings were beating the air, Caval's cloak was streaming out behind him, and he lowered his glittering rapier until it was pointing at Saraband's heart. 'I could kill you now, rat! But it is not the time, nor is it my destiny to end your miserable life. But you will die soon, Saraband. Very soon!'

With a triumphant screech, Tarquin soared into the sky. The stars were fading, but light still streamed from Caval's Sword. And, as Saraband realized whose weapon it was, he felt, for the first time, a tiny prickle of fear.

29 The Waiting's Over

Wild rumours were sweeping across Carminel. Every bird, every tiny creature, all whispered the same dreadful tales of Aramon in ruins, the Cardinal dead, Rufus and Elana slain by savage moles! In the Castle in the Marshes, the mice were close to despair.

But not Amren, or Seth. They steadfastly clung to their faith in the Lord of Light, and refused to believe that all was lost.

One morning, Seth helped Amren up to the battlements. The mild sunshine warmed their fur, and the air smelt sweet with the promise of spring.

In the high meadow beyond the encircling marsh, mice were hoeing and planting seed potatoes, runner beans, carrots and parsnips. But Amren knew that their hearts were not in their work. What was the point, when sooner or later the rats would turn their fury upon this, the last outpost of resistance to the all-conquering Saraband? Amren rested his paws on the warm stonework and sighed.

'Don't give in,' said Seth.

'I won't.' The old mouse smiled sadly. 'I just wish I could give them some hope. But we've heard nothing of Rufus, nothing from Odo; just these terrible rumours.' Amren would not speak of the fear that haunted him: that his beloved Elana might be dead.

Seth understood. 'Rumour feeds on bad things, never good. Why, if all these tales were true, Saraband would be here by now. But he ain't! So keep up your courage! You know the old saying: the darkest hour is always before –'

'The dawn. I know . . . Seth? What is it? What have you seen?'

Seth had seized Amren's paw, and the old mouse could feel that his friend was trembling with . . . dread? Excitement? 'Tell me!'

'Amren! The eagles! A great mass of them, flying

in from the east. And – and they're carrying mice! Hundreds of them!'

As Amren listened, he too could hear shouting and cheering growing louder. A sudden rush of air set his fur rippling, and his whiskers quivered to a warm, unfamiliar smell. Mice in the meadow were shouting too: a great cheer echoed round the courtyard as the Eagle Squadron landed in a flurry of wings.

'The mice are clambering down,' said Seth. 'There's Rufus!'

Suddenly, all was quiet. Seth let go of Amren's paw. The old mouse listened intently. Somebody was running up the steps and along the battlements to reach him. 'Who are you?' he whispered.

Warm arms encircled his neck, warm tears of joy splashed on his fur. 'It's me, Father! I've come home!'

'Feedin' yer face again, I see!'

After his imprisonment, McCrumb had been overjoyed to see Odo again, but he would not admit it to the Cardinal! Now, on the morning after their arrival at the castle, the cantankerous old mouse was glowering down at Odo, who was perched on a rock in the courtyard, contentedly munching rolls and honey.

'I'm making up for lost time!' exclaimed Odo. 'Or lost weight, rather. By the time the eagles rescued us, I was fading almost to nothing.' He grinned mischievously. 'What about you? Did they feed you well in prison?'

McCrumb nibbled his breakfast nut. 'I'll no' pretend the food was appetizing – but it was perfectly adequate for a soldier like me.'

Odo stifled his laughter. Ever since his part in the defence of Aramon, McCrumb had fancied himself as one of the Dirty Squad. He now wore a brace of pistols in his belt and lectured Finn on battle tactics whenever he had the chance.

'Well, *Captain* McCrumb, how did you enjoy your first eagle ride?'

McCrumb gave his tail a brisk, military flick. 'It was no' so bad, but I'd not want to make a habit of it. In the Dirty Squad, we fight on foot.'

Odo would never forget that wonderful evening when the sky had filled with eagles. Since leaving Aramon, the Cardinal and his band of refugees had trekked wearily from one farm to another, only to find them burnt and abandoned. For many days they had stumbled across blackened fields, with nothing to eat but the few tufts of grass that had escaped the rats' fury. For most of the time, they had lived on hope, but even that was running low. Odo knew that the eagles' rescue had come just in time to save them from starvation.

Beyond the castle, where the water-meadows sloped up to a ridge, Snout and his gang were on watch. Odo had told Finn how these children from the back alleys had scavenged for food in the woods, made stretchers from fallen branches for the sick and elderly, and had wandered far in search of water. Their reward was enrollment in the Dirty Squad. Now, they were taking turns with Finn's telescope to scour the surrounding countryside for any sign of the rats, for no one doubted that Saraband would come.

At first, Rufus had felt nervous about meeting the Cardinal, fearing that Odo would resent giving up his power. But, as they walked with Elana in the meadow below the castle, the Cardinal soon reassured him. 'My dear Rufus, I always believed that one day the King would return, and I am over-joyed that I have lived to see you! Now, when would you like to be crowned?'

'When we have beaten Saraband, your Eminence. Not before.'

The Cardinal was astonished. But Elana

understood. Rufus was determined to prove himself and earn his Crown in battle.

During those anxious days, Rufus seemed to be everywhere at once: organizing, praising, encouraging his mice. In case of a siege, he ordered the castle-mice to bring in all the food they could carry from the nearby farms. The country-mice gave it willingly, many coming themselves to join the army, and to give their families the protection of the castle.

Seth was delighted that the long wait was over; his secret store of weapons would soon be put to good use. He organized gangs of mice to fetch it, and the courtyard rang to the sound of his swiftly turning grinding-wheel, and sparks flew as the swords were sharpened to the keenest possible edge.

Days passed. Still no sign of the enemy . . . Until one bright morning, a shadow darkened the courtyard, and Juno almost fell out of the sky. Mice dashed to her side, as Bradwen tumbled to the ground, his tunic dark with blood.

'The rats! They've been marching by night and hiding by day! That's why we never saw them. I spotted them an hour or so ago. They were almost up to the river, where it flows narrow at the foot of a slope, west of here. They're about a day's march away!'

'Are you hurt?' asked Rufus.

'Just a few scratches. Juno took a bullet. I'll get Caval to see to her. We were flying low when Red Kites attacked us. I shot two of their rats, and Juno did for one of the Kites. The others chased us, but Juno outflew them.' Bradwen grinned at Rufus. 'It looks as if the waiting's over!'

After tending to Juno's wound, Caval wanted to send out another patrol. But Rufus forbade it. 'We nearly lost Juno and Bradwen. We'll need all your eagles and their riders for the coming battle. Burglar, tell Snout and his gang to keep out of sight and watch the rats. Let me know when they reach the river.'

All that day the mice stood to arms. The tension was almost unbearable. Then, as the shadows lengthened, a cry of alarm rang from the battlements, feet pounded over the drawbridge, and Snout and his gang tumbled into the castle. 'The rats! They're here!'

30 Council of War

The tension snapped. Mice, eager for battle, talked excitedly while they cleaned their swords. Rufus summoned his captains to a Council of War. They listened attentively to Snout's report.

'Looks like they've stopped for the night, just out of sight of here. Look –' Snatching paper and a stub of charcoal, Snout sketched a long ridge above a narrow river. 'They're up there, see; on the right, there's this wood, and on the left, the ground slopes away real steep. In front of this ridge, there's a long slope down to a river. Dunno what it's called . . .'

'The Collada River,' said Amren quietly.

Elana caught her breath. 'The same river that –'

'Yes. The same river where the rats defeated our armies long ago. And the same spot.'

The mice glanced fearfully at one another. Must they fight at such an ill-omened place? Rufus sensed their fear. 'It makes no odds. I'm glad Saraband's chosen the Collada River. It gives us a chance to avenge that defeat. We shall wipe out its shame for ever! Snout, how many rats are there?'

'Hundreds! And their priests are there too, leapin' about an' casting spells on us! You should've heard them.'

'That won't harm us!' exclaimed Odo stoutly. 'The Lord of Light is our protector!'

'You've done well, Snout,' said Rufus. 'See that your section has something to eat, then get some rest. I may need you again later.'

For a long time, the mice pored over the map. 'Are they intending to stay there?' asked Odo. 'Or will they advance and attack the castle?'

'I don't know,' said Caval. 'But if we are to have any hope of beating them, we should attack them where they are. The castle walls aren't strong enough to withstand a really determined assault.'

'Where would we make our stand?' asked Odo.

None of the mice doubted that they would have to fight but, despite Rufus's brave words, the odds were fearful and every mouse knew it.

Caval pointed to the map. 'See where the ground slopes gently to the river? We'd have to take up a position just this side of it. Might give us some protection . . .'

'Sure, an' if we do that,' said Finn, 'the scumbags'll simply pick us off with their rifles – and us not able to fire a shot in return! Thanks to Seth, we all have swords, but only Caval's Squadron have pistols.'

'We have the eagles!' exclaimed Amren.

'And the Treasures,' said the Cardinal, with a grin at Rufus.

Caval shook his head. 'I know we have the Treasures, but none of us knows exactly what they will do. We have fifty eagles, and as many riders, who might drive some of the rats away. But the Red Kites could be a problem.' He looked bleakly round the table. 'Many mice would die.'

All eyes turned to Rufus. 'Well, Lord King?' asked Odo.

Rufus left the table and stood by the window, gazing down at the courtyard. Peace-loving mice, turned soldiers, sat talking quietly, while their children played in the evening sunshine. Old mice puffed their pipes and wondered if peace would ever return to Carminel. These are my mice, thought Rufus. Their lives hang on what I decide, and if I get it wrong . . . He suddenly felt very lonely.

Elana came and stood beside him. Her smile made Rufus realize that he was not alone. Confidence returned. Suddenly, a plan took shape. He turned away from the window and saw the others watching him, waiting patiently for his decision. 'I think Saraband wants us to attack. So we will . . . Tonight! We'll leave the castle after midnight, take up a position by the river, and cross it before dawn. I know these rats: they fight fiercely, but they like their sleep. And they'll be over-confident. If we attack while it's still dark, the rats won't realize how few we really are, and Caval's eagles will be twice as frightening by night.'

So it was decided. But Caval's words, 'Many mice would die', still echoed in Rufus's head. While Finn set about organizing the mice into groups, Rufus went to the kitchens, where he found Snout and his gang.

'How fast can you run?'

'We's champion sprinters, sir!'

Rufus grinned. 'This won't be a sprint, more of a

213

cross-country. Now listen carefully. The fate of Carminel depends on you. Here's what I want you to do . . .'

31 The Reaper's Blade

Only the old and the very young stayed behind.
Amren stood at the castle gateway and blessed the
mice as they marched boldly into the darkness to
face an enemy many times their number.

The Eagle Squadron had already flown to the
hills behind the enemy's line. There, they would
wait for the mice to attack before making their own
deadly charge.

Finn and Rufus were leading the way, with Seth
to guide them through the marsh. The mice
marched in silence. All weapons were muffled in

cloaks or sacking, but the tramp of so many feet sounded horribly loud. At last, after hours of weary marching, a long, dark line loomed on the horizon: the ridge, where the unsuspecting rats lay fast asleep.

Every mouse knew where to go. Rufus, with Seth, commanded the left wing; Burglar, Dead-Eye and Silence led the centre. Finn and Odo led their group to the right, from where they could see the dark smudge of woodland that marked the extreme left of the rats' line. Elana, clutching the Chalice, went with them; so did McCrumb, who was confidently expecting disaster but had insisted on coming just the same.

Crawling on their stomachs, the mice inched forward until they were lying among the tall reeds that fringed the stream. 'If only the night were not so clear,' whispered the Cardinal. 'To advance, even in the dark, will be risky.'

'Och, the whole thing's risky!' hissed McCrumb. 'Strategically unsound! Now, what we really ought to be doing is –'

'Look!' Elana was staring at the Chalice, from which a thin tendril of mist was slowly trickling. As the mice watched, the mist curled along the stream. Gradually it thickened, until the whole army was shrouded in a milky vapour that stretched a hundred paces or more behind them. 'You were saying, McCrumb?' grinned the Cardinal. But for once, McCrumb was lost for words.

As the mist rolled over him, Rufus took out the Crown. Silver light gleamed from the ruby, making the mist seem denser than ever.

From the distant woods, a bird chirped. A gentle breeze sprang up. Slowly, the mist began to roll forwards, up the slope, until it smothered the long ridge from end to end. But the way up the slope was clear.

A faint light was glimmering in the eastern sky. 'Pass the word,' whispered Rufus. 'Advance!'

As the message flashed along the line, mice touched their swords for luck, murmured a prayer to the Lord of Light, and crept forward. They waded the icy stream. Hardly daring to breathe, they climbed the slope.

They halted at the crest. The rats were invisible, but their stench was strong! Rufus raised the crown. Waves of blood-red light flowed out. From the far end of the line, silver light from the Chalice gleamed in reply. All eyes were on Rufus. He drew his sword. 'Follow me!'

His mice charged after him, checked as they

stumbled over the sleeping rats, then swept on. Woken by the sudden clash of arms and the cries of the wounded, the rats groped desperately for weapons. But the line of mice was like the reaper's blade.

Saraband erupted from his tent, and saw ghostly shapes running towards him through the mist. 'Get back!' he screamed. 'Fight, you miserable cowards!' The rats hesitated but, as Saraband hurtled towards them, snarling curses, they swung round and followed him, crashing into the advancing mice. Red Kites circled the battle, squawking loudly, but unable to see a thing.

And now came the eagles! While Bradwen, with half the Squadron, swooped on the Red Kites, Caval drew Gideon's Sword, brandished it, and raised it high. His eagles swung into arrowhead-formation and a dart of light flashed from the Sword, spreading across the sky until the fading stars looked pale.

Caval swept the Sword down. Instantly its light pierced the mist, and the rats hid their eyes, crying in terror as the Eagle Squadron wheeled into the charge! Rapiers flickering, talons gleaming, they swooped on the rats. The Squadron soared into the sky, circled the battle, then down they swept once more.

Bradwen's eagles were hunting the Red Kites. Seeing the rats falling back in disarray, the birds tried to escape. But one by one the Red Kites were hunted down and destroyed.

From behind Saraband's tent, Kei the raven poked out his head. He stared in terror at the battle. Gunsmoke, mingling with the mist, dried his throat and made his eyes water. Above the warriors' heads, he could see the lurid gleams of light from Crown and Chalice flickering across the field. Kei shrank back in alarm. There was no escape. The eagles were sweeping the field in charge after charge.

The raven glanced round at his little squad. 'Come on, lads,' he croaked. 'It ain't safe 'ere. Let's go for them woods.'

Keeping well clear of the battle, the ravens scuttled for the woods on the far left of the rats' line. They sheltered among the branches, quaking at the dreadful din of battle and the triumphant yells of those terrible mice.

As the mist dispersed and the sun rose, the rats began to realize just how small an army was attacking them. Taking heart, the warriors began to push the mice back towards the crest. In the centre of the field, Saraband was yelling excitedly. He had picked out the leaders, Dead-Eye, Silence and

Burglar. He was hacking his way through so that he could have the pleasure of killing them, when a cloak of darkness fell across the battlefield.

Saraband glanced at the sun. A silver star was passing in front of it. Gradually, the sunlight faded until only the star's light remained.

32 Duel of the Gods

The sounds of battle died away. Everyone stared in awe at the star. Strangely, although its rays were streaming across the sky, the battlefield remained shrouded in darkness. Suddenly, Saraband remembered the prophecy of Morvan, the High Priest.

> 'You will rule in the Mouse-Lord's Hall,
> Until by daylight stars shall fall;
> And darkness hide the morning skies,
> And from the west the sun shall rise.'

Daylight had indeed turned to darkness! 'Back!' cried Saraband. But even as the rats turned to follow him, a star-beam shot to earth. Saraband screamed in terror. He saw another sun, its rippling rays rising from the ground and a long line of shadowy figures, stretching right across the battlefield, cutting off the rats' retreat. The Mould-Warp had come!

In the centre stood Rothgar, with Wiglaff beside him. Summoned by Snout and his gang, they had marched all night. Rothgar raised his axe. The moles advanced. Above them waved Rothgar's personal banner: the sun in splendour!

A rat was running past. Saraband grabbed him. 'What direction is that?'

'Left,' said Nym.

'No, you blithering idiot! Is it north, east or what?'

'West, I think. Can I go now? Skills is dead,' he added miserably. 'I don't reckon the Sable Lord wants us to win this battle. He's deserted us. Look at them ruddy earth-shovellers and their fancy flag! We'll never get past them!'

The moles were closing in. Desperately, Saraband fought his rising panic. 'No falling stars yet!' he screamed.

'Oh, no?' asked Nym. 'What's that, then?'

Distant flickers of silver were falling from the sky. They were Bradwen's eagles, only their wing-tips visible in the gloom as they returned to the battle – but it was enough for Saraband. All Morvan's prophecies had come true.

Rufus scented victory. As he held the Crown high, golden light flowed from the ruby and mingled with the silver beams from the star. 'Come on! Follow me!'

The mice cheered and surged forward. Caval's Sword was a beacon of light as again his eagles swooped from the sky, driving the terrified rats right on to the advancing moles. Swords and axes rose and fell, gleaming as the star's light grew ever stronger.

Gobtooth, fighting savagely, was yelling to the Sable Lord. Other warriors took up the cry, 'Reveal yourself, O, Sable Lord!'

'Saraband! Get away while you can!' cried Morvan, but Saraband gripped him by the throat and shook him until his teeth rattled.

'You and your prophecies! No, I will not run away! The Sable Lord will not let me die! I'm going to kill that accursed slave and get the Crown!'

'Let – me – go!' squawked Morvan. He pointed a claw at the sky. A dark cloud was swirling overhead.

Thunder roared, savage streaks of lightning stabbed the earth. Saraband stared in wonder at the thing that was taking shape above the battle.

Reptilian scales shimmered, from the top of its dragon head to the tips of its forked tail. Red eyes gleamed, and huge, spikey wings slowly beat the air.

Rufus watched in fascinated horror as the Sable Lord slowly circled the battlefield: then, it spotted the Crown, and dived. Forcing down his terror, Rufus raised the Crown like a shield, his paws trembling as dart after dart of blood-red light shot from the ruby. The Sable Lord screamed, but still its eyes blazed at Rufus, and it swooped towards the mouse until its great body filled the sky.

Star-beams lanced down. Gaping, sizzling holes appeared in the Sable Lord's wings. The Dark God screamed in agony, swerved aside, and soared towards the star.

The battle on the ground was forgotten. All eyes were fixed on the duel of the gods. Angry red beams flickered from the Sable Lord's eyes and shot from its spikey wing-tips, but they were instantly quenched in the constant silver streams flooding from the star.

Still the Dark God fought on, streaking across

the sky, raking the star with its piercing darts. It seemed that nothing could kill it. As Rufus watched, some instinct sounded a warning. He swung round. Saraband was striding towards him.

'So, little slave! Our god is fighting for us! You and your miserable mice are going to die! And I'm going to take that Crown you stole. It's mine!'

Once, Rufus might have been afraid of Saraband. But not now. He turned to Seth, who had remained close to him throughout the battle.

'Seth! Take the Crown while I deal with this vermin. Don't be afraid. Its power will guard us both. Now, Saraband,' he snarled, 'in your pride and ambition, you ignored the ancient prophecy that when Carminel is in peril, the eagles will fly and a King will arise! The Crown is mine! I am King of Carminel and you are finished!'

Saraband was thunderstruck. 'You – the King? I don't believe it! You were born a slave, and you'll die one!'

Seth had given Rufus his best sword. But Rufus nearly lost it as Saraband's savage cut hacked down on the blade. The rat was incredibly strong, cutting and lunging with bewildering speed. Rufus parried as best he could. But, step by step, Saraband was driving him back. With a sudden turn of his wrist,

Saraband sent Rufus's sword skimming across the grass, and the rat's sword-point was at his throat.

Suddenly, Saraband vanished under a pile of mice as Snout and his gang hurled him into the mud. They tried to grab his sword, but Saraband was too strong for them. He flung them aside. But high above the battle, Caval had seen what was happening. Like a bolt of lightning, Tarquin dived, until he was hovering over Rufus, and above the wild beating of the eagle's wings, Caval yelled, 'Rufus! Catch!'

Rufus reached out. Gideon's Sword fell into his paw. Saraband flinched as light flashed from the blade, but he returned to the attack, hacking and cursing. A voice spoke sharply in Rufus's head: 'This is my Sword, so use it well! Parry right – now left – good! He's raising his sword – lunge – go on! Lunge now!'

Rufus flung himself forward. Saraband, his sword upraised for the death-stroke, collapsed without a sound.

The Sable Lord screamed in mortal agony as a star-beam pierced its heart. Its body shrank until it was no bigger than a rat, then, with a high, thin wail of despair, it vanished.

Suddenly it was all over. The rats groaned and

flung down their weapons. 'What shall we do with 'em, sir?' asked Finn.

'Round them up. Our mice and eagles will escort them to the coast. They must return to the land they came from and never trouble us again.'

'Right, you rats!' cried Finn. 'You heard his majesty! It's back overseas for you! Oh no, you don't!' he snarled, as Kei and his band attempted to sidle out of the wood to freedom. 'You're going with them!'

Rufus held out his paws gratefully to Snout and his gang. But, to his embarrassment, the little mice knelt before him in the mud.

From all over the battlefield, through the dust and smoke, mice and moles were making their way towards Rufus. There was McCrumb, limping proudly from a leg wound, eyes sparkling behind his spectacles; Wiglaff, overjoyed that the moles had come in time to help his friends, and Elana, still holding the Chalice, her eyes fixed on Rufus.

Suddenly, great shadows loomed overhead, and the Eagle Squadron swooped to the ground. Bradwen leapt from Juno's back, strode up to Rufus, and seized his paw. 'You've done it, Rufus!'

Rufus shook his head. 'It was the mice, the moles, the eagles and the Treasures. Not me.'

'But you made it happen,' said Caval. 'You found the Treasures, and they gave us courage. You called the moles, and they came. For you. You gave us hope, and made us believe we could do it. It's your victory, Rufus.'

Seth, who had been proudly guarding the Crown, returned it to Rufus. 'Lord Caval's right! You did it – and now you really are the King!'

'King Rufus of Carminel!' smiled Odo. 'And when we return to Aramon, my dear friend Amren shall crown you in the Great Cathedral!'

Rufus turned to Elana. 'I can't manage it alone . . . Will you help?'

Elana felt as if her heart would burst. 'Yes!'

Rufus felt better. But, as he gazed out over the battlefield, he saw the dead. 'Oh, Lord of Light!' he cried. 'Let there be no more killing!'

'They died for what they believed in,' said Cardinal Odo quietly. 'We shall remember them. All of them.'

The Crown shed a soft golden light over the battlefield, and a voice that seemed to come from the star whispered,

'The souls of the dead live in peace on my Island,

No more misery, sorrow or death shall they
  see.
Now govern my creatures with justice and
  mercy –
A glorious King in a land that is free!'